Was it Me ?

MARGARET BALDOCK

Was it Me ?

Margaret Baldock

The right of Margaret Baldock to be identified as the author and illustrator of this work has been asserted by her in accordance with the Copyright, Designs and Patents Act 1988.

First Edition Printed 2019

Text and Illustrations © Margaret Baldock 2019

All rights reserved. This publication may not be held on any retrieval system, broadcast or transmitted in any form whatsoever, or any part of this book be transmitted electronically, mechanically, photocopied, recorded or otherwise without the written consent of the owner.

ISBN: 9781092185219

DEDICATION

"To Home"

Most of my stories end up in my beautiful Wales, (although this one started in Euston Station London).

Maybe it takes me back in time and I remember old landmarks in deep forests, rusted wonky gates held together with twine and a bit of faith, they were past their best even then, but with another pull and a push and perhaps a lift they became manageable again and opened with ease until the next time. Old boulders that seemed bigger once, but on returning, they were only vaguely recognizable, almost lost, covered over with *time* and moss, and everyone knows that time waits for no man. So with all these thoughts and snippets accumulated in a box lost in *time*, I put pen to paper and continue, and then I stopped with this one at the end of Greg's journey.

Please read and enjoy "Was it Me?"

Margaret B

CONTENTS

1 Was it me ? 1

2 Greg's story 4

3 Foster 6

4 The Three Vagabonds 7

5 Pills, what pills ? 9

6 He had to go back, and soon… 11

7 "Can I help you, young sir ?" 14

8 The open road and the year 1992 16

9 This was a new day 18

10 The little lady 20

11 Brutus 22

12 He will explore 25

13 "Breakfast, young man" 27

14 Days turned into weeks 30

15 In the meantime 31

16 The past, the present and the future 32

17 Home 34

18 Foster homes, and Yes ! 35

19 Past, present and future 37

20 Busy time ahead 39

21 Work, work, work 42

22 Barry's place 43

23 Glamour; with a chink in its armour 44

24 Winter 48

25 Barry stuck and in trouble 49

26 "Man caught in snowdrift" 51

27 Spring 52

28 Gilbert 53

29 Rubbish 56

30 Something blue 57

31 Elsa 60

32 Springs turned into summers 61

33 October 62

34 The party 64

35 Thoughts and schemes 66

36 The day of the exhibition 68

37 The party 71

38 Promises 73

39 London 77

40 Monday morning 81

41 The city was not for him 82

About the Author 90

SYNOPSIS

This story came to me when I noticed two Buskers on the street in London. I was sitting in Euston Station having a drink in a bar waiting for my train to take me back to Wales.

Alongside the boy and girl was a street artist who had no connection at all to the others, he was quietly sketching people that passed by, and had quite an audience. I noticed how quickly he sketched, therefore, as fast as he drew the more money he made, and so I went across to W H Smiths and bought a small writing pad to take notes. I had no idea what I wanted to jot down on my writing pad but there was something about the three neighbours that stood alongside each other maybe their unkempt hippy look compelled me to make notes.

Distracted for a moment I left my briefcase on the floor and crossed over to Greg's the Bakery, then a policeman came running after me to ask if the bag was mine, no one had touched it and I was an object of an alert as it might contain a bomb. After a brief explanation that they were just orders and invoices, I picked up my bag and was about to walk away when the young girl singer bumped into me, her hazy/tired eyes met mine, and just then I saw the character Mel.

That was many years ago, and the memory and notes were stored. So, this inspired me to write this short story, Was It Me

Greg and his mother lived with Grandad in a small terraced house; Grandma had died several years ago. So, they lived there after his mother gave birth to Greg, but when he was very small, she died from an overdose of pills, depression was the word he heard.

Grandad could not cope with bringing up the child alone and married for the second time. , but the new woman did not take to Greg, and from then on, Greg was left to his own devices, and was fostered time and time again. Eventually, at the age of sixteen, he left his last foster home and met up with Mel and Ross. Mel was the singer and Ross a guitarist and writer, both were into drugs, more to sell than to take.

Soon, the three Vagabonds made their way together on the streets selling whatever substance they could. Singing and drawing as they went from place to place in Greg's old V W camper, who he named Jerky Jenny, as the girls he invited in were usually quite accommodating.

The old mattress that the threesome had to bunk on when there was nowhere else to sleep had many uses, and entertaining an attractive female was high on his agenda.

One evening when they had more than enough to drink, they headed back to where they had made their temporary home, when Greg who was driving felt a bump.

Had he hit something...a child maybe?

He was distraught with worry and this was the turning point in his life.

He left the twosome that night with just enough cash in their secret place to go on without him.

He headed ...in any direction that was out of town, and found himself in Wales, where he pulled up in what he thought was an old gate entrance leading nowhere, 'he thought', and there he fell asleep.

There was a sharp tap on the window and a small, white haired lady looked over the rim and asked him to move so that she could get the gate open to go to her farm down the lane.

Greg helped her open the twisted gate that she had to lift before it moved, it was obviously too heavy for her to manage. Then without thought and a quick glance she asked him if he wanted some casual work as he didn't seem to be going anywhere in particular.

And so this is how Greg's story goes...it develops into a solid friendship between a young boy and a middle aged little lady, things worked out well for them both but not without obstacles as you can imagine...otherwise there would be no beginning, no middle and no ending to this lovely tale.

Funny Sad and exciting, read on and enjoy Greg's Story.

Margaret B
Teller of tales and author of "Was It Me?"

1 WAS IT ME ?

It had been one of those hot sultry days, August 1972, and Greg was celebrating his twentieth birthday with a couple of bottles of beer and a packet of chocolate biscuits stolen from the new supermarket across the way from where he and his two friends Mel and Ross had marked their pitch for the day. They were down 'nd outers like him, misfits in this world of many in similar situations.

The three vagabonds were buskers and did what they had to do in order to get that ready meal, usually a Big Mack or some fish and chips, best bought at the end of the day when Louise Burger bar and chippy on the corner was clearing out the odds and ends from the greasy fryer where he would scoop out the crispy batter fish bits and charred chips. A few of their fellow buskers pick pockets and street artists had sussed this routine out too, but these three had become firm favourites with Louis the proprietor, therefore a few extra bits were saved on the side for them.

They had been living in this area for quite a while and, so far so good, no-one had interfered too much in their affairs. Their affairs, as Ross called it 'business', was drugs and pills. Nothing too harmful but, never the less, it was enough for the punters to return and the cash they made was enough to keep them going from day to day. So the quantity they sold was limited to each person so as not to draw attention to themselves by overselling.

After quite a profitable day, and a few more beers, Greg and his friends drove through the run- down council estate where the houses were boarded up to keep out unwanted squatters and vermin that mingled with each other. Recognizing and respecting their own private space, they were rife in a place like this from stray dogs and cats to the occasional interloper that dossed down for the night.

Over loaded dust bins and bags filled with God knows what, ripped to shreds by dogs and cats alike, enjoying the remains of the curry left from last night's meal and the night before that congealed with soggy bread and discarded buns and the accumulated magazines that were women's lifeline in between changing of the overfilled nappies, that had long since turned a baby's bum pink with urine.

They turned the last corner into their estate.

Most of the properties on this run down almost forgotten place were far from secure. Broken doors, leaky roofs and broken windows that would never mend, and easily accessible with a turn of a screw.

The flat that Greg, Ross and Mel occupied was on the first floor of a high-rise block of flats which they had easily entered with the aid of a crow bar and a hammer, now locked with their own security system of barbed wire and a lock that didn't lock but was there as a deterrent for effect and a bit of luck. That was the key to their home.

This was a neglected part of town where the copper on the beat would never go on his own fearing any repercussions from a drunk with a knife if he dares to disturb his sleep. But, for now, this small unwanted flat was an unoccupied space and it was theirs, a place where they would eat drink and be merry for their short stay. All too soon the police would move them on to another town another place and a chance to score again, but so far they had lived in this squat in peaceful existence for some while, even to the point that the few other squatters in the block became neighbours and customers who would drop in for a chat and a line or two of coke.

They were well accustomed with the pattern and warnings of the impending police presence. Sometimes a wolf whistle from the ones in the top floor flat to tell them to take the bits of washing in that they had draped over the landing rail or the electricity cable that was fed from the landing plug through the letter box and into the T V and cooker. Then each in turn would switch their man-made system off and remain quiet, just like turning the Christmas lights off in town.

One move in the wrong direction and then the holler of "Oh Bloody hell" then you knew that someone was in a shocking state having tried to repair or reconnect a bare wire, but it was the chance you had to take to survive. There was no water supply apart from a bent pipe somewhere on the ground floor and turned on and off with a spanner. If they had to exit, they would scarper just like rats down the hole and scurried with no trace, other than tell-tale silver paper, a fine knife and a baked bean tin that was half empty and spilled.

Forewarned by a friend of a friend of the pending police raid they would pick up their goods and move quickly and stealthily to make their get-away. Sometimes the three of them slept in the old V W camper that Greg called his own 'Jerky Jenny', named after a rather sweet girl that was quite accommodating for a while then like most of the other equally accommodating girls was dismissed of her favours and forgotten ...time to move on before they wanted more than a quick jerk on his comfortable old mattress.

Greg was a free spirit; he was tall and his hair was sometimes the colour of gold but sometimes it was a mousy colour depending on how often he managed to have a wash, but underneath all the grime he was a good looking boy with the most beautiful blue eyes that drew you into his world and closer to him. He was devoted and trustworthy, and had learned to take care of himself and his friends if ever they needed his help.

Marriage or any other encumbrance was not on his list, and many a serious suggestion by a lovesick follower was out of the old V W pretty quick, and then Greg would be on his way again. But, for a good while now these three had been pals, Ross shacked up with Mel on a permanent basis, and Greg did what he had to do with any pretty Jenny that happened to pass by his old wagon.

2 GREG'S STORY

As a child he lived with his mother and his grandfather. He never met his father, never knew he existed until he was told sometime later that there was a father, a scoundrel, a good for nothing layabout who stood no chance of going straight. Always the little guy on the outside of a big robbery never the big time Mr Big. The last to make his getaway suspected of being involved in all that was crooked, and disappointed that he was not in with the big boys, always the look-out always the looser, and sometimes a policeman's nark if he was hard up. But then Greg was too young to understand much about fathers and mothers only to know that Grandad doubled up as both grandad and Dad.

When Greg's mother became seriously ill with something called depression (not that Greg knew what depression meant back then) but on that one dark day she was gone. Suicide they said, not that he knew that word either, but he did remember that he cried a lot, when one morning she was not there in her usual chair staring into space as she usually did. Then half-heartedly she would make him some breakfast still looking blankly ahead or through the window. But that morning it was just him and grandad.

Grandad remarried soon after, but his heart wasn't in living, especially with Hilda, who was the spur of the lonely moment thought. Or a promise he made in the pub. Then Grandad died. His wife, Auntie Hilda, had made both their lives a misery with her constant moaning and her demand for more money. Enough was never enough for her, and now there was no comforting shoulder for Greg to cry on. Then she ceased to be nice to Greg, not that she was that nice to him from the start, she showed a little love when others were around but failed on the sympathy score, and her understanding of a child's distress was not recognised. She did not understand why he cried a lot and told him to shape up and be a man, but

Greg's world was shattered with almost one blow. Mother gone and shortly after so did Grandad, with no ceremony, no grief just a piss-up in the local pub where Hilda flirted with Sam the chef, who soon moved in with her and slept in a brand-new bed 'specially bought for the occasion.

Gone were the framed photos on the old dresser of past times good or bad and Grandad's wedding photo, there was no sign at all of his mother or his Grandfather apart from one snap of happier days on a beach in Wales, which Greg rescued before the next bin day came 'round. Instead of the memorabilia that once were there, on the table in the hall, and the small crochet tray cloth with its fruit bowl that was always empty unless Grandad had thrown some screws in, in came a new telephone table with an attached mock velvet seat in green that took pride and place with the new green trim phone to match.

Things were looking good for Hilda and her new man as there had been a small pay out from the insurance that Grandad had kept going for years. Too soon the small terrace house that had been kept clean and tidy turned into a gaudy pub, bedecked in cheap shoddy plastic furniture, with a bar straight out of HAWAI FIVE O. Flashing lights and various cocktails and shakers ready to make up any delight that their cheap friends would imbibe.

Dear Grand 'ma, poor Grandad, and his mum were gone, and as the tears flowed down Greg's red cheeks when he often thought of his mother, he no longer had a family, no one to call his own.

Locked in his room for hours, listening to the thump-thump from the bedroom next door and fed when she pleased, he became withdrawn, sometimes he would escape through the window and onto the sink/tin roof, then the short drop from the drain-pipe would do it, and he was out until it was dark looking out for any scraps that were left, then he'd sneak back up the stairs and back onto his well-worn mattress and thin cover that was once his grandad's.

 She entertained new admirers some that enjoyed the pleasures of her body when Sam was at work and some that were there for the incessant music and drink that went on all day and every day almost, until the neighbours had enough then the Rozzers (Police) were called. She blamed Greg of course for wandering in the streets and drawing attention to himself so that the police would bring him back.

Greg was left to his own devices.

Until the day when he was found wandering outside the house in the rain wearing just a tee shirt and a pair of wellies that he had managed to pull on, he was almost six and wasn't clued up yet about left and right feet, the left wellie was on the right and the right on the left. He was soon picked up by the authorities and the rest is history …as they say. Not that Hilda cared a monkey's chuff about him, he was just an extra nuisance, and now she could take in a lodger that would pay a decent price for his room.

3 FOSTER

From then on Greg was passed from one foster home to another and had almost lost count of the families that had eagerly welcomed him, and then realized that he didn't fit it with their life style. He was quiet, withdrawn and sat alone for hours with a pad and pencil drawing twisted faces, black twisted trees and twisting roads that went on to … nowhere just a bend in the distance then nothing more, maybe it was a reflection of his life maybe he wanted to take a look around that bend.

Mr and Mrs Stewart were probably the best and the last.

Greg was ten at the time. No children of their own and they lived in suburbia where each and every house was kept neat and tidy where everyone kept up with or beyond the Jones' and beyond their means. They were pretty posh, were the Stewarts, with high standards and high-priced clothes. The child was lonely and needy but they were too busy with their committees and golf club activities to notice the sad little boy that sat in his room with the sketch pad and pencil.

Therefore, one day Greg wrote a nice neat note of thanks, and a drawing of a young lad walking away down a long dark and winding road…

At that age of sixteen, he moved out, and moved on with friends and acquaintances in a similar situation yet again they were not family they were good time friends who shared their ill-gotten gains and the loot they stole on route. Then one day along came Mel at first, looking for company and someone to talk to, and for a while she shared his mattress but not his body, they were just friends that looked out for each other she was dodging and dealing and he was sketching and watching, until Ross walked by with his guitar over his shoulder and joined them, he played his guitar with melodies that were equal to any professional guitarist, so now the group was complete.

4 THE THREE VAGABONDS

Mel was the watcher and singer, (when she was in the mood) most of the time she was lost in her own world of coloured pills and pretty flowers but if she put her mind to it she was not a bad poet and she often read her poems to passers-by. Then her words were put to music by Ross if he could be bothered and Mel sang, while Greg drew.

Mel and Ross were a well-matched pair and in their own way they were in love, he turned a blind eye to her thieving besides she was good at it and very often came back with an unexpected delicacy that otherwise they would not have and eating was high on their agenda. Mel's streaked hair was tied in a plait then pushed out of the way into a very expensive beanie hat, a neat scrunched up item that she acquired on her way round the high street, somehow it found its way into her big overcoat coat pocket which was always full, with sweets and some make up (acquired).

Greg sketched, he was an artist although he had not recognized his talent, to him it was a means to an end. He drew faces in the crowd then, just as they were near enough, he would show them what he had drawn and enticed them to have a quick caricature drawn. Sometimes a young man would come along with a photo of his girl-friend and wanted a 'proper' one drawn not a sketch but a nice one to give to her as a surprise.

His talent and accuracy surprised the punters; some would want him to draw a child or a dog, which he drew perfectly, tweaking a little if a young boy was not the most photogenic, or an impatient girl who wanted to be on her way to the toy shop, her parents were delighted with the enhanced results and would come again with yet another member of the family or friend. A small crowd of people would gather curious to see the finished product. So, their money pot was always full, as Mel warbled to Greg's drawing and Ross would quietly strum, eventually breaking into a solo piece.

Young ladies would come to talk, loving the attention from both boys, Ross giving them the sly look of a Lothario and Greg using the aloof attack that brought them back for more, keen to be taken inside the old van and see more drawings, maybe sit on his mattress for a while. But Greg was rather picky about his women and his V W camper which sometimes doubled up as his home; this was his private place; therefore, his lady friends were few and far between.

Mel would talk to the women that wanted a sketch or a drawing done, and would coo at a blubbering child that seemed appeased when she produced a sweet from her Mary Poppins coat, that held everything other than the kitchen sink, and so Greg was able to draw a relatively good likeness, as the infant chomped on a jelly baby. Then, Mel would smile politely at the mother who handed over her money and admired the likeness of the child that Greg had drawn.

There were some incidents, during the course of their life on the road and one almost led to Greg ending up in casualty.

One such young lady who Greg took a shine to was married, she was bored with her role as a new housewife and frequented the square they were working in. She sat in a coffee house opposite the trio and fell in love with the handsome Greg. She invited him to have a cup of coffee with her and soon after he invited her to see his drawings. But, a dutiful friend of a friend conveyed the message to the husband who then scrawled on the side of the V W, the words 'you wife stealer and get out of town you B..... before I break your arms' and other expletives that were painted on the side of the bedroom scene. So, with a few strokes the words Jerky Jenny became a pattern of letters on the side, as a reminded of his great escape.

But scrawls and words were soon mended and psychedelic art replaced the green and yellow sign of The Vagabonds and only the J Jen', remained with colourful squiggles that meant nothing to anyone other than themselves. The trio left the patch the following day so as not to make a fuss, they did not want to draw attention to themselves or taken in by the cops...no way.

The incident was soon forgotten, along with what's her name???

5 PILLS, WHAT PILLS ?

On this warm sultry Saturday evening the three buskers drove through the littered covered streets of broken bottles and dirty nappies. Greg failed to see what was in his way. A thud, then Mel's scream shot through the van disturbing their laughter and song. They had sold most of their gear of hash and pills and were in good spirits and Greg although not a heavy drinker, and as it was his birthday, had been persuaded to have that 'One More', even though he was the driver.

The shock stopped their merriment or perhaps it stopped the drinking for a moment or two, then Greg muttered, "What was that, shall I get out and take a look, what the hell do you think it is"?

"Don't be so silly Greg" came Ross's garbled remark "You'll be shot at dawn with so much hooch in your body and some gear in the back, and what about the rest of us? We'll go down too if it's anything other than a dust bin lid"

Mel sat in the back perfectly still, except when the bump in the road sent her flying and her small thin body sprung up from her seat and her heart thundering, but she still giggled.

"Go back later Greg if you must but it will be something that an idiot has left in the street an old tyre or a dust bin lid, so drive on for 'Gawd' sake, - Drive on".

However, Greg was not happy with her suggestions; it was a thud more than a clang, but what sense could she make of it …she was almost out of it. He will go back later what if it's a human being, a child? After-all there were a few out at night half clothed running free or running scared in the street, while parents were too busy watching some- thing on T.V. a game show or Life on the Dole. Nursing a bottle of cool lager and a packet of fags, child forgotten by the time the second and third bottle was open.

Greg knew the feeling well and remembered the day when he was left alone in Grandad's house, despaired and frightened.

6 HE HAD TO GO BACK, AND SOON…

Jerky Jenny came to a stop inside their bat-cave (garage). They hurriedly took out their stash and ran inside with their hard-earned wages stored in Greg's sketch pad, and they made to their hideout.

Yes, he must go back.

"Milk that's what we didn't get" Greg said.

Mel. she had done her best with the shopping that she had acquired before the sales person came round the isle again, but her pockets were full and the obvious bulge of a milk carton would show if she took just that one more thing.

"I'll nip to the corner shop, won't be long"

Greg was certainly the only one with a conscience.

He had always wondered why he had been deserted all those years ago. He had never caused any trouble and was a very good boy as far as he knew, but how he had ended up in care he had no idea. He was honest (to a degree but that was more from need than greed) food and shelter was the order of the day, existing was a must, and he rarely took a drink and certainly did not partake of any substance other than the odd smoke or two, depending on the company.

He was a handsome boy and very likeable, besides he was a nice guy, and always kept himself tidy and clean, that is why he was usually the one to go to the corner shop. His hair was cut to an obedient style, short back and sides, while the other two vagabonds were eyed with suspicion, their dread locks chains and tattoo's took up most parts of their body and gave them that 'don't care attitude', their shifty-ness made them look totally untrustworthy, Mel and Ross were, as they say, two of a kind. While Greg was a bit of a loner. But they got on well together as a team of modern-day vagabonds and thieves, so he went to the shop.

There were two others ahead of him at the counter a burly man with a scruffy beard. He wore a vest that was stained with the dribble of gravy, over his portly frame, which hardly measured up to the over stretched fabric with a noticeable hole underarm where it had worn to a shred. His tracksuit bottoms were of an eggshell blue colour, glossy and stained. He smelled of nicotine and stale onions. The other person in the queue had a child in her arms, and the conversation was about a boy, the hit and run and the driver that did not stop.

"Shame" said the woman with the child, "He was left alone in the 'ouse for hours and wandered out. He went to look for his mother, four years old and out in the street, lived three doors from me" She tutted, as she shuffled her child from one arm to the other to count the small change she had in her purse, and cursed him when he wouldn't stay still in the awkward position.

The man with the beard agreed with the woman and left with his purchase of four cans of beer and a bar of chocolate, not forgetting the fags.

Greg approached the counter, "What child, and where did this happen?"

The man behind the counter said that it was just a few streets away. "A hit and run apparently", and took Greg's money and handed him the milk and served the next customer.

Greg froze to the spot and a few seconds later he quickly left, he could not think straight and wanted to leave before he looked guilty or concerned. The effects of the day's booze had not quite worn off and now he was shaking from the worry, and the conversation.

'Shall I go back through the road or shall I take the short cut through the gap to avoid the place where I felt the bump?'

He avoided it and scrambled through the small gap in the hedge and into the park. Someone called out 'Hi Greg' but he hurried on, passed the broken prams and window panes.

That's it! he decided. He was going to hit the road. Just Jerky Jenny and me he thought, we will start again a life on the open road; a turning point ….no more drugs no more dealing, and no more drink.

But first he must go to the Cop Shop to confess, maybe! But at least to find out if it was him that had caused the accident.

When they had eaten their fish and chips and counted their money they prepared to sleep. Mel was fast asleep in no time and Ross cuddled up to her, pressed hard into her back. They were unperturbed by the incident but then they were not the driver, and the driver only had a provisional licence slightly altered and screwed up into an illegible worn out piece of paper, unrecognizable as a licence.

It was time to go, Greg quietly picked up his quilt, his bed, his blanket and few possessions rolled up in a bag. Travelling light, instant departure was part of their lives, their familiar game was to pack up quickly and run.

This time he decided to go alone, although he did not like to leave his chums. But there was no turning back, this time he was going; and so, he left a note written on the scrunched-up chip wrappers.

It simply read, going, going, gone. Money in the hole where we left it. Taken enough to fill up with fuel and a bit for my travel …good Luck.

He was a little sad and guilty, they had been together for almost two years as a team, but Ross and Mel were a couple and they would make their way in the world, her voice and his guitar and the drugs, besides there was quite a bit of cash left for them stashed in their hidey hole.

7 "CAN I HELP YOU, YOUNG SIR ?"

The officer behind the desk was drinking his tea, eating a large pie, and scrutinizing his magazine of naked women. Nothing much happened in the small police station, and he hardly noticed Greg, who by now was thinking of turning back.

"Can I help you, young sir," came the voice from behind the mag.

Greg was doomed, trapped, he had to explain.

"Well…err, I've had an accident, and I want to report it please".

Just then the phone rang and the rather large officer rose from his well-worn chair and slowly made his way to the back office and turned his back on Greg, now was his chance to leave…But.

"Just a minute I'll answer this"

Greg shuffled; he wished he had not come in 'shall I leave while his back is turned?

"The hit and run you say" the officer glanced towards Greg "Drunk, yes I see, good –good, caught him trying to leave was he?" and put the phone down.

He repeated the conversation to Greg.

"Nasty accident on the estate last night, hit and run child out in the street and a lunatic in his fast car tried to get away from the cops, no chance" ….

Greg heard the words LAST NIGHT, and knew that it wasn't him. FAST CAR, certainly not him, Jenny was never fast, and she just trundled along at her own slow pace and gasped if Greg tried to push her to a higher level. He had not killed or maimed or caused the accident, in fact he was miles away the previous night wooing and drinking with an old acquaintance and did not get back till dawn.

"Now young sir, what can I do for you?"

Greg handed him a wallet "Found it in the street by the chip shop, not much in it, but there you are"

It contained a fiver that he had in his own wallet. He was going straight, him and Jerky Jenny heading for the open road…

It wasn't him after all.

8 THE OPEN ROAD AND THE YEAR 1992

What lies ahead for us now old girl? He patted the old van's bonnet as he made his way to the driver's seat. He glanced at his well-worn tyres and wondered about his tax disc that was forged, easy work for Greg. He could work wonders with a pen but one day he will be caught, till then he lived on a knife edge, hope and luck.

To stop at the police station – what was he thinking of, and Jenny his little heap almost crippled and worn out?

Let's get out of here, pretty quick old girl.

It was late on this Saturday night, it remained warm and humid as Greg drove out of town. Suddenly, realizing he was alone, his quiet mood and no singing or Mel's laughter, no guitar and he was lonely. He took out the photo of his mother that was a curled up amongst his drawings. Soon he would not be able to keep it safe, it might get lost in the rest of his muddled world of crayons and brushes, that one day when they gather their things and go, and his memories would fall out of his folder, lost on the breeze.

Greg never felt so alone as he did at this moment.

Should he go back, it wasn't too late to turn back. They may not have noticed he'd gone but his tyres bothered him, perhaps he could get a job, pay for new tyres, get a new life, but soon dismissed that foolish idea.

After a while of constant driving he was well out of the town that he had become familiar with, he was heading for the country and must have been driving for a couple or three hours or more when he found himself somewhere in quieter surroundings, he was ready to sleep tired from the day`s upheaval and trauma.

His eyes were closing, concentration gone, and fatigue taking over, so he pulled into a side road where he would be concealed from the main road and the police. There he stayed 'till the next morning curled up in the back of the old VW. Snug as a bug, but where was he going, what road was he on? As dawn broke he looked out onto open fields and the smell of fresh air and grass that slightly mingled with the weed.

There were cows in the field close by quietly grazing and a bit curious when Greg nipped over the gate for a wee and wash his face in the stream where some other cows stood and drank from the same stream just some paces up from him. Greg cleaned his teeth in the water that they shared, and as he straightened from a crouch position a big black face, pink nose and extra-large eyes looked straight at him from the opposite side eager to lick the toothbrush he had in his hand.

Greg laughed and decided that he had done the right thing, the countryside and the smell of cows appealed much more than the grimy city pavements where he sat all day sketching.

9 THIS WAS A NEW DAY

There must be somewhere along here, a shop a café or something where he could get something to eat. He was hungry and had not thought of food until now, last night's fish and chips would not last forever and a cup of coffee would be welcome, he needed something strong and black. He realised that he had to get back onto the main road before he found anywhere, this road seemed to be heading for the hills and there would be no shops up there but then he had to keep his head down, as the defects on the old jalopy would one day be revealed.

There was no traffic on the road, Sunday morning most people would be resting or cleaning their cars, mowing the lawns, or recovering from the night before… Mr Stewart cleaned the car every Sunday morning, and Mrs Stewart peeped through the curtain just in case she missed something that was going on in the avenue. Greg was not included in this ritual, so he got on with his homework and Lego.

He pulled into a lay-by some way down the road where a man was opening up his gleaming Buffet-Bar', there was a smell of fresh coffee and he was eating a sausage sandwich.

"Where are you off to lad" said the chap known as Barry the owner of this small palace. Did Greg want to get involved in conversation especially when he didn't know where he was going himself.

"On the way to visit friends they moved on before me, down to Mid-wales somewhere, no rush I will catch up with them sometime"

Then he looked at the sign on 'Barry's best beef burger /mobile café'.

'Rhandir- Mwyn' Farm, he tried to make out the words, he must have travelled further from Birmingham than he thought, and he was in Wales already.

"Any jobs going 'round here do you think? Anything will do". Then he took a chance – farm there must be some jobs.

"Labouring? Something, anything maybe?"

He didn't want to sound too keen, but he did need to get the old V W off the road.

Barry rubbed his greasy hands on his nice clean apron, and realised that the boy meant farm work but was not sure enough about Greg's motives and eyed him with suspicion. Was he a traveller looking for friends, a chancer, a thief? He knew that he was clever enough to have noticed the sign on the van and had taken the opportunity to ask.

"Perhaps we can give you some work back at the farm, if you want to stay around for a while come back later and I'll speak to Rose-Ann" I'll get her down here to show you the way to the house she's quite busy just now ... the hay and all that."

Rose- Ann eh!

Maybe a quick roll in the hay, with a buxom bit' who knows'.

Greg pulled away from the buffet-bar, sausage sandwich half eaten and coffee drank, he waved thanks to Barry just as he noticed the police car that passed by so he turned 'round and headed for the hills.

Jerky Jenny was unused to the twists and turns of the narrow lanes and the sheep that just wandered casually across from one field to another, from the side of the road and into the path of the traffic if there had been any traffic except for the old VW's cough and the loud engine, the creak of the gears as she stumbled on obediently to Greg's gentle foot on the accelerator. But it was otherwise silent; there was no rush for them to get across it seemed, and the look which definitely said "Wait young man, no hurry" and carried on grazing, before stepping out in front of him.

He reached the top of the hill, mountains and small dwellings right there scattered in ones and two's with acres of land between and a view to die for, all was well in Greg's world, and folded the creased photo of his mother back in his folder.

He pulled up in a gateway, it was neither a path, nor a road, as far as he could tell it was just a track. Then he laid back in his seat and admired the view before him, he felt like a King surveying his land and again he fell asleep.

10 THE LITTLE LADY

There was a tap on the window and Greg woke up with a start. A small white-haired lady about 5ft tall looked in over the rim and exclaimed that she wanted him to move so that she could go home, and pointed down the track.

"What are you doing here anyhow?" she said, "Up to no good, youngster?"

Greg was surprised to see a human being in such a remote place. There was no sign of life down the track other than a couple of horses in the field, and the track seemed to go on for miles, where was she going, did she live alone down there maybe she had a large family, how lovely he thought.

She struggled with the heavy gate that was stuck and needed repairing, it was covered with grass that had wound itself round the edge preventing it from opening fully and a large stone that had nudged itself off the wall which she tried to move, and so Greg went out to help her. She asked again what was he doing in such a quiet place and somehow Greg wanted to tell her what had happened the night before but who was she?

She drove on through and stopped to push the rusty gate but not before Greg asked her where Rhandir Mwyn Farm was, or some name that sounded like that.

"Looking for work are you lad? I've got a spot of painting and tidying to do round the old place, bed breakfast and meals thrown in what do you say?"

He instantly liked the rounded, middle aged little lady and said that he had to go back to the roadside café and tell Barry that he would take up her offer, besides she seemed to require more help than him who could fend for himself and looked like an affluent gent'.

The gate was the first thing in need of repair.

Barry's café was closed when he got back, so he left a note 'thanks for the offer of a job but I'm moving on', and off he went up the winding road again and closed the gate behind him. It started to rain, and the mist was coming in over the mountain. The gate was heavy; A job for tomorrow.

It must have been about half a mile down the track to the house and as he made it round the bend there it was. Perfect in every way, a picture post card with roses round the porch climbing on to the roof and upstairs windows.

"Who lives in a house like this?" he thought, "Wow"! But she was right; it did need a spot of paint and a tidy.

He could see immediately that the garage/barn door was off its hinges the outhouses could do with a bit of a spruce up and a paint job, other than that on first glance it was perfect.

She greeted him at the door with a smile that could light any dark day, and as the drizzly rain fell it beamed a halo across the doorway,

He liked this old place, and he liked the little woman.
"C'mon in lad" she smiled, "haven't had anyone here for a while".

11 BRUTUS

The big Alsatian dog greeted him too with a leap across his chest that could easily knock down a giant. Another 'something' sort of a dog jumped down off a cosy chair and rubbed his nose against Greg's leg waiting for his turn to greet him. "Brutus... Max? Meet the boy".

He was offered a cup of tea, which she poured from a shiny blue teapot that matched the two cups; there was a cake and fresh bread and butter. She did not wait for his answer, she assumed that every young man was hungry, he must be hungry and a large thick piece of fruit cake was placed on a blue plate.

"I'll show you around the ol' homestead when you've had a bite to eat and a change of clothes; I gather you have a change of clothes? And while you take a bath those can go in the wash; they'll be dry in no time in this weather".

Greg was taken aback by her generosity, she had no idea who he was, and he had no idea who she was either, but a sort of trust came across from one to the other. Too soon to accept so much, he thought, but there was a niff in the air. He could smell the underarm odour, and that was certainly a bad sign, the brook where he had washed his face earlier and shared with the black/white cow who had taken her fill higher up the stream, and left him with the dirty pond water, would not have been classed as a wash.

Too much of Jerky Jenny and his young conquest a few nights ago too much drink, and no hot water, besides his impromptu decision to leave left him no time to wash.

What was her motive? Why the rush to take him in? Was it safe to be there?

The dog! One command and he was sure he would be at his throat, but there was no denying ...he was smelly, he was dirty. He took up her offer, thinking to himself that he was the fittest of the two humans, but the dog!

...well he seemed to be trained to kill but it was a chance he had to take for a fresher Greg.

It was a marvellous old bath, antique as far as he could tell. It matched the rest of the bathroom perfectly with its blue and white Wedgwood coloured tiles and the whitest towels ever seen, the floorboards scrubbed almost white to match. A couple of other fresh white towels were left on the side of the bath for him to use and his old worn out bag was left outside the door, he hoped she wasn't going to lock him in after all, and that the dog was not going to stand guard outside in case he tried to get away.

No, it was not a part from a film he had seen where a writer had his legs broken and kept prisoner. This was real and he was in it.

A small window was partly open onto a sloping roof, this would be no problem for a getaway and as Greg looked out, he could see the sea in the far distance, and another long lane that obviously led away from the farm. This house was built on a rock, with the views of the mountains on one side, the sea and even a town or city on the other.

However, there was work to be done; Tomorrow.

The old mongrel dog Max was waiting for him outside the bathroom door lying lazily on his bag smelling the old fish and chip smell that lingered...he was in doggy heaven.

"Max" she called out to the mutt, "c'mon. Leave the youngster alone", that is when Greg realised that they had not yet exchanged names, but the dog Max was friendly enough.

"Mari" she said in a broad welsh accent, "Mary to you I s'pose, and you?"

"Greg short for Gregory I s'pose", they appreciated each other's sense of humour, and an understanding was immediately struck between young and old.

"Shall I show you around the old place then?" she asked; keen to show him her little empire and surrounding land. "Shall we start at the top and work backwards?"

They walked slowly back up the track from where Greg and she had met. The Alsatian remained close to her heels, and she pointed to the acres of land that were hers. She pointed to the horses in the field; "they belong to a young girl called Sarah about your age I think, eighteen, or nineteen? She rents these front fields, does a lot of show-jumping and competes in all the local shows. No doubt you will meet her if you stick around".

Greg was tall for his age but had a very boyish face so could be mistaken for a younger lad, and with the clean fresh air and the clean sun-bleached golden hair, well who knows what lies ahead. The open air had done him good and did she really hope that he would 'stick around'. He did not tell her that he had just turned twenty a few days ago in fact he had forgotten it already, but he would like to 'stick around' if only to help her with the work that needed doing. They reached the gate, and she mentioned the latch and the rusty hinges that needed repairing, "Heavy old thing this gate and as you get older, the gate gets heavier, have a go tomorrow will you Greg?"

They turned around and walked slowly back, Greg admired the view the mountains and the forest, and he inquired about Barry, the farms and surrounding area. Mari didn't disclose much about Barry and said that he owned the nearest farm to hers but that was two miles away, and that he was very wealthy.

"He wanted to buy some of my land some while back. Then I discovered that he wanted to put caravans there, a blot on the landscape as far as I'm concerned, what do you think youngster?"

Max walked alongside Greg, as close as he could.

"He's taken a shine to you," Mari said and forgot about the answer.

The bigger dog, the Alsatian Brutus, stayed close to her watching her every move, looking after her as he always had, it seemed, and the bond between them was undeniably a strong one.

"Let's go on my boy see what needs doing and when you've seen enough come on in, there will be some home-made ham for tea"

What sort of world was he in, what sort of gentle woman was she?

Around the back of the house was an orchard where freshly washed sheets where billowing in the breeze, like parachutes pegged out to get the maximum of wind just like a wind-sock on an airfield; they would be dry in no time. The sun was warm again and he felt his cheeks tingle from the sensation of its rays.

There were six ewes in the lower field. They came towards Greg and sniffed his hand as they mingled together with two goats jostling for a position in his hand. There were three cows, a dozen or more hens in the small yard, and a hen-coupe close to a hedge. Beyond were acres more land stretching for miles and the track that he had seen in the distance went down towards the town and through the forest in a long meandering curve.

12 HE WILL EXPLORE

An avenue of fir trees stood on both sides of the track a short distance from the house and beyond those trees there was a dense forest, where there had been some tree felling, old trees perhaps.

He did not go into the outhouses, besides there was so much to see, the garage door that was off its hinge and the paint work. There was certainly more than enough for Greg to do for a while, that is if he stayed around and more-so how long did she want him to stay?

She called his name and whistled to the dogs, this pattern of calling them back to the house was soon to become familiar to him, a comforting sound a request not a demand. He went back to the orchard and gathered in the clean fresh laundry. It seemed to be the natural thing to do. Dinner was served on old willow pattern plates; the old scrubbed table was white with age and wear. New potatoes, some tomatoes and the succulent ham, cooked to perfection. Max the mongrel sat beside him and waited; he had tasted her ham before.

When had she prepared such a feast he thought, and the homemade wine? What a treat.

"Gooseberry wine" she said, "very potent, mother's recipe". Mari had tasted this once or twice before just a sample of course.

They ate their meal; they drank the wine from almost transparent old cranberry/red coloured glasses and went through a list of what he might do tomorrow, unless she had other plans for him. He would start at the top of the track; the big gate was priority as it was too heavy for her to open and close. All too soon the day was done and Mari offered him the choice of three vacant bedrooms, hers was the fourth the last and the biggest at the end of the landing.

Greg declined the offer of the room and said that he would prefer to sleep in his old V W. He had a good but well-worn mattress and he was used to his familiar surroundings; it was warm and cosy. She was not to worry about him and thanked her for her hospitality; he would be up early to start. She brought down a large quilt from one of the rooms and a pillow with a cover as white as snow. There was a white sheet to put on his mattress and she took his old quilt away. He was sure that it would be in the wash tomorrow. But what! Why the generosity?

Max laid down close to him in the van and they both snored their way through the night.

He was not up that early the following day, however he was greeted by the galloping Alsatian Brutus who had made his way into the van via the part open door that was ajar because of the soaring heat; it was another hot day. Then there was a shrill whistle and the call for Brutus to come, and instantly he was there at her feet looking up adoringly at his mistress.

Greg emerged to see Mari, washed dressed and waiting by the door. His old quilt must have been in the bin it was past its best anyway and might have died of shock to find itself in the washing machine; it would have disintegrated and torn by the sudden suds of cleanliness... besides it did smell peculiar.

13 "BREAKFAST, YOUNG MAN"

He washed and shaved in the lovely bathroom and looked out onto the slate roof, and with one glance the memory of the old corrugated roof from his childhood was gone in a trice. he came down the narrow stairs to the big kitchen where Mari had prepared breakfast. It was a feast with lots of fresh tea from the blue teapot. However, he did notice that she had several similar blue teapots on the top shelf of the old dresser, and then curiosity got the better of him so he asked her why she had so many.

"One for best" she said "one for using, one for the electricity money, and heating, one for savings, and one for a rainy day" she laughed, "there might be a rainy day, but not today it's much too sunny".

There was a gentle warning in her voice as she revealed where her savings and rainy-day money was. There for the taking if he had a mind to cut and run.

"Trust...me boy", she said, "It's all done on trust"

The dogs were fed and the chickens too, the goat was milked, and the cows were waiting patiently for their turn as she showed Greg how to do it. Badly at first but he soon got the hang of things. Soon after this new experience Greg placed some tools in a wheelbarrow and headed up towards the big gate. Max went with him, but the big solid Brutus stayed in the yard close to Mari.

There was a young girl in the field; he presumed that it was Sarah as she tended to her horses. He went over to her and explained who he was and why he was there in Mari's house, just in case Sarah thought that he was an interloper, but that was hardly likely as Max stood close by. She was happy with his explanation and said that she would look in on Mari when she had seen to her horses. Was she going to see if Mari was alright and get the story straight from her? Maybe!

Greg started to work, and as he cleared the grass and brambles from around the rock and big boulder that held the gate, he did find a name at last; the house was called 'Y Graig' (The Rock). Very apt for such a house that was perched so high amongst the rocks and almost touched the sky. There was also a post box, nothing inside only the remnants of an old nest. Soon the task was completed, after some squeaking and tweaking, the stones and well embedded grass and moss was removed, and the gate swung open with ease.

Sarah followed down to the house soon after, on the pretence that she would come by tomorrow to drop the rent money off for the field. Mari introduced her to Greg and gave her the full story of how they met and how much she needed some help around the place, and if she would like to drop by she was most welcome to have tea with them anytime.

She could see that Sarah was concerned about this young man's appearance out of nowhere, and that Mari was to get in touch by phone if she needed anything.

Very diplomatic Greg thought. Of course, you could trust no-one these days and he had just turned up out of the blue. Later that day Mari showed him the barns and the outhouses. The dairy was the one nearest to the house and next was a converted smaller room; that was her loom/spinning room where she had stacks upon stacks of wool packed in polythene and cardboard boxes, and an old spinning wheel passed down over the years but still worked to Mari's orders and nimble feet.

"Not bothered with it for years" she said as she sat on her favourite little stool almost as if she was ready to begin spinning again. It seemed to be a hint for Greg to tidy this place up a bit, but what a waste. There were knitted gloves scarves, and beautiful jumpers stacked and labelled neatly packed in rows in polythene bags.

"Maybe we could look through it tomorrow?"

"But maybe", Greg said in a ghostly rat like voice "they will all be full of rats and mice that have made their nests inside over the past years, but then just maybe we could salvage the best"

Mari hadn't thought of rats in her little den. But then Mari hadn't been in there for ages, the cobwebs on the beams overhead had weaved their magic webs of fine lace but the tell-tale absent minded fly had not heeded the warning and was dragged into that comfortable resting place, it was a web to be avoided...

But maybe things could be done with a lick of paint and a broom.

"The children used to come up from the local schools on one or two days a week to learn how to knit and use the spinning wheel and to turn the fleece into wool. We had angora rabbits then and mother and I spun the most delicate jumpers. They were good times; Mother was alive and father too. But cut-backs and the icy cold winter weather prevented the children from coming. The roads were blocked and impassable so the children never came. Then they held classes in the library and swimming in the new Swimming Pool instead. New glamourous young teachers went their own way with other ideas, as the high heeled brigade could not conquer the gate or the rocky road to the house.

So why did she stay …here alone so far from anywhere, no corner shops, no cinemas and no rowdy bars and drunks. She wasn't young perhaps in her sixties, but then that's not old and she was as agile as any teenager. What was behind that kind smile, was she sad, why hadn't she married. He presumed that she had not married, and lived with her parents all her life, but he told himself to mind his own business, if she wanted him to know then she will tell him and like-wise his business was his own.

14 DAYS TURNED INTO WEEKS

He painted doors and sheds and repaired gates and walls, he milked the cows and fed the chickens. He left the goats to Mari as he had already felt the kick on his shin when he tried to do it. There must have been a gentler way of milking goats or maybe they preferred her way to his and told him so.

He had been at the farm for over a month, autumn was on its way and it would get colder in the old van, so he plucked up the courage to ask if he could sleep in the house. Nothing had been said about moving on, and now that the basic repairs were done there was nothing to keep him there. Should he tell her that he should be leaving should he leave, was she expecting that one sentence 'I should be going?'

Mari had gone down to the village so… he would speak to her when she comes back.

15 IN THE MEANTIME

Greg took some time to walk down the track, down towards the forest on the other side of the hill; there were a couple of miles of walking ahead. Max as always was there at his side and went along to keep him company. They walked a crooked mile till they came round a bend and a very large rusty gate ahead, similar to the one on the other side of the hill but this one had not been opened for many lead onto what seemed a main road, this is where they stopped.

The gate had not been used for years by the looks of things; there was a rusty chain that locked with an equally rusty padlock. The name of the house was hardly recognized, just a crooked piece of wood that had Y Gra... written on it and presumed to be the same name as the one on the other track but beyond the gate was a main road which led down to a town and beyond that was the sea. It was a car drive away.

Was all this woodland hers too?

16 THE PAST, THE PRESENT AND THE FUTURE

He had not talked much about his past, the drugs, the quick exit from the estate, his friends. As far as Mari knew he was just out of Art College and wandering from place to place as most kids did these days, he had touched lightly on his life in foster homes, and said that someday he would like to settle down and have a family.

She had not pressed him for more.

Likewise, he had not intruded on her life, not once had asked if she had been married, widowed or never married, and she didn't volunteer any information.

Yet, he did feel that she wanted to talk and tell.

Mari had not returned when he arrived back at the house, so after a quick cup of tea he went to the back of his van J Jen as he called her.

He took out his sketchpad and charcoal sticks. He had not had any time to draw since he had arrived and missed his old sketch pad and pens, but there was so much to see, so much to sketch up here amongst the clouds and peace, the scenery and the animals were his models.

So, he sat down on the low wall near the front of the house. Max remained close, so he started with him. A dog lying on an old shoe peacefully dozing waiting for his tea. Then the garden and the house with its perfect chocolate box features, its uneven walls and tiled roof of different blues and greens replaced with new over the years. The upstairs windows freshly painted and the old washbasin that he drew from memory almost sepia brown in the bedroom window. Greg could improve and enhance any picture, but this was perfect.

The outline of the house came to him easily. He would like to draw the inside too with the rocking chair by the fire and the old scrubbed table. But that was Mari's home, inside was her domain and he would not impose. It was her life with its private corners. He realised how much he had missed his sketching and drawing, and soon he had something that resembled a nice piece of art.

There was the sound of a car coming down the drive Mari was back, what would she think of his work, after all 'he had been to art school…not' so she would not be surprised to see him sketching.

"Wonderful, just great" she said looking over his shoulder, burdened down with a large shopping bag.

"Wasted, that's what you are me boy, you must do something with your skill as an artist, But I have been thinking about things, what we could do, here with this place, now that it's tidy"

He was perplexed, and wondered what it might be as he went to help her with the shopping she had brought up from the village.

She might have come to the same conclusion, was it time for him to go did she want to put it up for sale, or was it that he was not needed any more, so was it time to move on?

17 HOME

"How do you feel about staying here permanently, Greg?" She paused, making sure not to meet his eyes. It was a delicate subject and rejection would have been an embarrassment for fear that he would have misread the invitation. Then she went on, "Perhaps we could do something with this old place, the barns and a couple of the cow sheds could be renovated? We could start a school again, and convert the old place into holiday cottages; they seem to be all the rage now. What do you think? Oh! That is if you'd like to stay"

There! She had said her piece, and poured the hot water into the blue everyday pot, and carried on as if she had not spoken.

He was speechless, but she continued "Perhaps we should talk a bit more eh! Tell me about yourself, and I will tell you a bit about me"

Should he tell her all about himself, Greg Mason, thief, vagabond homeless, where there any good qualities that she had obviously seen in him, where his beginning and where would it end?

18 FOSTER HOMES, AND YES !

He could draw and paint, she knew that much; did she have a sixth sense? She was no fool, no pushover that's for sure, but she did trust him he realised that, but what did she want. Was she more devious than he thought, would she turn him into her slave with her guard-dog watching his every move, will she tell him the truth about herself?

After all no-one from his old life knew he was there, or anywhere else for that matter.

He could find out more about Mari for himself if he went down to the village or the town- but what about trust, she had mentioned her rainy day savings so she trusted him…as if he was her own son. He could have walked away pockets bulging, but she trusted him. Dinner was served almost in an awkward silence; one of them would open the conversation? The chores were done the washing up and the animals were settled for the night and now it was the quiet time. Then they sat outside in the orchard, Greg sketched again, he felt safe and relaxed with his pad and pencil, a barrier between him and the conversation that was to come.

She produced some writing material she had purchased in the village.

"I knew you could draw Greg, I went inside your van looking for any dirty clothes and found your folder with the sketches, smells a bit of something nasty in there me boy, must clean it out, what do you say? The old thing could do with a bit of a spruce up; although you can use the Jeep once we've sorted out a few things eh? If the constabulary came up here, they might look at the Tax and insurance too, you do have insurance Greg, and the tyres?

She had sussed him out fair and square…"

Now tell me your life story truthfully"

Before he had realised, he was telling all, his childhood as he wanted to remember it, and yes! For a short while he went to Art School, but then left as the stress of bullying became unbearable and the rest is as she saw it, was history.

"Tough times, eh lad?" she patted his shoulder.

He almost cried, but held it together, and turned away to pat the dog that shared his sadness, and licked his hand. He was glad to get it over and done with, a burden shared with a little welsh lady, who wanted to share her story with him too. She opened a bottle of homemade nettle wine. It seemed the obvious answer to start the ball rolling and loosen the tongue. There was a hint of sadness in her voice, and then she started.

19 PAST, PRESENT AND FUTURE

She had lived in the farm for most of her life, then went to college and became a teacher. She went to work in London attracted by bright lights and adventure of a big city, but too soon after falling in love with a scoundrel who spent her hard earned cash she discovered that she was pregnant and when he had beaten her badly enough to miscarry the child she returned home and tried her hand at farming, then knitting and teaching again. As time went by and her parents died, she was left with the farm and therefore her teaching had to be set aside. But, as time went by, the gates needed repairing, and umpteen other things needed attention. She knew that she could not manage the bigger things alone, and so did Barry from Rhandir- Mwyn. He knew that it would only be a matter of time before she needed some help with the animals, and started the ball rolling by offering to buy the top field, and perhaps later he would have offered to buy some more of her land...at a favourable price of course.

But she knew that he had plans to buy the farm, when and if she was ready to sell.

She digressed, but soon regained her thoughts,

"The child would have been forty years old now" she sobbed.

"Loved children" she said, and hid the sadness in her eyes with her embroidered hanky.

Greg patted her shoulder.

"And you, young man, tell me more, is there anything I should know...drugs drink robbery"?

Greg poured himself another large glass, the wine was sweet and heady and as planned it made talking much easier.

"Nothing that should worry you Mari, the usual a bit of drugs and a little bit of stealing to stay alive, a few beers to take away the pain of the past, so I hit the road leaving the past behind me and found you and this place a second chance one might say. So, shall we say we have a deal, we'll do the best we can with the homestead eh! Just remember I only have my two hands and a bit of muscle to give, money I have none".

They agreed to their plan and would talk again in the morning:

Mari was up early the next day, and sitting at the table with her cup of tea,

She was drawing up a plan of the farm where the cars would park and accommodation for holidays. She had some good ideas but not well planned. She was so excited, but her so called sketching's were just OK, and Greg glanced over her shoulder, then when he added a little more design to them, they resembled a plan, "not a bad drawing but are you getting ahead of yourself?

"I suppose we need architects and surveyors so we will put some ideas together to show we mean business".

Greg took over, and drew the barns and the old stable.

Do we need to go to the bank first"?

"All done yesterday me boy in the hope that you would not turn me down".

They were now a team of two, and to seal their friendship and understanding, they had some more wine. Money! That was the question and how to broach the subject, was there enough to start with and how would they make some more to keep going as it was going to be some project.

"Don't you worry about that" she said smiling and tapped the side of her nose "I have some loose change in my tea-pot".

"Need more than loose change Mari, and how much do you think this little lot will cost, although if we get the barns done, things will slide into place. Trial and error and a great deal of faith that's all we need".

20 BUSY TIME AHEAD

This was it, there was work to do and in order to get the ball rolling they decided to start on the barn, cleaning and destroying, throwing away any unwanted rubbish. Then the re-furbishing could start with a clean slate, split it into three and there you have it. Three two bedroomed cottages. Then there was the old loft where the farm help or shepherds used to sleep, the old cement and brick steps leading to it, but that will remain as store room for a while. Plans were put in place, although Mari remembered that there was an old plan already passed for some alterations as they wanted to extend some parts of the barn when they ran the school, so with a nip and a tuck these were presented once more with a wink in the right places and quickly passed.

Truckloads of sand and cement came rolling down the drive, and a couple of men were employed to help with the build. Then one day when the work was well on its way, Barry the hot dog /sausage sandwich man came to call, and with him came his daughter Rose Ann. A big girl to say the least, with boobs that took up most of her body, and arms as thick as a weightlifter, she was without doubt ... fat.

The roll in the hay was certainly dismissed.

Greg watched both father and daughter slide out from the massive land cruiser that was, quite frankly, made to fit their shape and size. Anything smaller and it would have crumpled under the weight, too many beef burgers; Greg thought. Barry emerged and greeted Mari with a hug that threw her off her tiny feet and took her by surprise, not having been greeted in this way by him before. What was all this about Greg thought?

"Heard about your plans Mari, what's going on then, the old place needed a bit of a spruce but a business venture at your age. My goodness do you think you can manage it all yourself"

"I'm not doing it by myself Barry, meet my right-hand man and partner

Greg. I believe you've met before,"

Greg reached out to shake his hand; but it was not a friendly gesture as Barry condescendingly shook Greg's.

"How did you find your way here youngster, aiming for a little lady living alone were you"?

Greg drew his hand away, as Mari interrupted.

"You'll be disappointed to know that Greg is a friend's grandson from my college days. She passed away last year and Greg found some old photos, and then found me to break the news of her death in America.

There that should do it! No names no address, America and any enquiry he'd like to make was far enough away from Wales.

"What"! Greg thought aghast at such blatant lies, told so smoothly, so convincingly by this little lady with a smug smile on her face, "and of course he is here to stay she added".

"Just wondered about the top field Mari, I'd like to help...maybe buy it, there would be plenty of money to finish the job in hand and you'll need plenty to get on with such a project. What do ya say? Then we'd spread a bit to get access to your farm from mine, a new road to tie us both in and make a go of it caravans and a toilet block, what an idea there would be no stopping us Mari".

Barry was on a roll and thinking of the profits and owning the land, but he seemed bewildered and concerned by the sudden arrival of this total stranger that could get in the way of his plans. But there was a stop to his ideas and she dismissed his plans, but said that she would think about what he had said.

"Oh! By the way I've adopted Greg legally and binding; a bit old for adoption but then with younger hands and mind I think we will make it together"

What the hell is she saying and so convincingly that Greg almost believed her; he must have a word when they've gone.

"Don't forget to close the gate Barry; we don't want just any old rouge dropping by"

Thank goodness he's gone, now for a strong cup of tea and a piece of cake...and an explanation I suppose.

I really don't know what got into me Greg, it was there on my lips and I had to say it."

"Never liked the man anyway, or his daughter come to that, perhaps he was aiming for marriage...you and Rose eh Greg?, then he would have access to the farm as I have nobody else to leave it to so I must make it legal and binding to you if anything happens to me ... adoption I think, if it's possible. Shame I had to lie about my so-called friend, but someone there in the heaven above spoke to me, and as I don't have a son of my own then I had to steal someone else's and you seemed to fit the bill. Do you believe in fate Greg, or was it luck that brought you to my gate?"

21 WORK, WORK, WORK

Soon most of it was done, the cottages were prepared for letting and a young girl called Elsa was employed to clean and tidy each weekend.

But Barry was causing a bit of a nuisance. Determined to be part of the action, he opened the wall that separated the two boundaries, and invited overnight campers in on to his land. One at first then three or four tents emerged on the hill overlooking Mari's farm. It was going to be a difficult situation as Barry had not thought of providing toilet facilities. No water other than the stream that flowed close to the wall on Mari's field, and this is where they came to fill their cans with the clear water straight off the mountains, and climbing over the wall to use Mari's newly built toilet facilities.

When Greg approached the visitors though, he was surprised to be told that the farm owner, Mr Barry Wright, had given them permission to use the facilities located just on the outer edge close to the barns and a short walk from the edge of the field. Of course, these people had no idea that they did not have such permission from the actual owner, and that Mr Wright did not own the fields, but what could they do about this awkward situation. Mari was not one to cause a ruckus.

A personal call on Barry would be the best solution, she thought resolve any misunderstanding then he will build the wall back up again and stop this nonsense.

22 BARRY'S PLACE

Greg offered to go with her to Barry's place but as she had known him for most of her life as a neighbour and his parents too, she was quite keen to go it alone in the hope that he would be reasonable, she would be fine on her own, besides; Brutus will go along for the ride.

She was in for an unpleasant surprise.

As she approached the long drive, adorned with two stone lions one on each side of the entrance, a large foreboding heavy metal gate faced her, with the initials B in gold on one part of the gate and the letter W on the other side. Very ostentatious to say the least, and out of sync with the rest of the landscape. As she came close, a box on the wall screeched a loud alarm sound to say they she was too close to the gate, which made her wonder why such security.

Gone was the old wooden gate that was perfectly adequate for a farm entrance, this replacement in black and gold was a blot on the landscape, totally out of character with the surrounding hillside and green forest. What would his step-father have said if he was alive, he certainly would not have approved of such a monster?

A voice came from the box placed on the wall, "Move forward, now", Barry's recorded voice came booming from an intercom just like a Hollywood movie, and then the gates opened slowly to let her pass through, and equally as slow it closed behind her.

Brutus did not like it, it squeaked a little.

Not so perfectly executed after all.

23 GLAMOUR; WITH A CHINK IN ITS ARMOUR

The long drive was smartly re-surfaced. She remembered it as a farm track where walkers could walk freely and horses cantered down towards the next field and the one after. It was once similar to her own rocky and bumpy road. If you drove the old Forde tractor too fast you would be shaken to the core and it caused you to leap off the old metal seat if you drove too fast. It was good fun when you were a child, but now the fun had gone out of the rocky road.

My goodness, the front porch and the once old-fashioned entrance was gone, replaced with a large wooden door with an elaborate brass ship's bell with clanging chain that would be loud enough to wake any sleepy soul and send them leaping out of bed. Glass panels with ornate filigree shapes of a tree and a serpent climbing up, and on the other side was another panel with a similar tree and the serpent heading downwards. What a statement piece of opulence. What gaudiness and bad taste she thought.

Two more stone lions with unfriendly and scarred features, with gold chains and medallions around their necks, sat on guard each side of the entrance. The old farm was beginning to look like a mansion, brightly painted and overdone with chintzy curtains.

'Barry must have some money', Mari reckoned, although his step-father was not that well off back then. Just an ordinary sheep farmer who loved a pint and loved to stop by the gate with her father as he passed by in his old jalopy, sometimes they would find time to chat for a while putting the world to rights and discuss the farms down the road, and whatever next was to happen in the village.

The first Mrs Wright (Sadie) used to come by often too, sometimes helped with the knitting, but then one day she did not turn up and soon after, there was a new woman in the house with Barry her son, who Mr Wright adopted as his own.

But where was Sadie?

There was talk that this new woman had been on the scene for some time, worked at the local pub and John Wright was smitten, caught with his trousers down, so poor Mrs Wright was out of her mind with worry, speculations and gossip was rife in the village close by that she had fallen into a state of despair and muddled, and that she had been put in a home for her own safety. Mari remembered very little of the scandal that surrounded the incident as she was away in London at the time, but soon just like most things it became yesterday's news.

Mari noticed the brand-new Jag in the drive, and another foreign car, gleaming red with it bared chrome teeth, it was an angry looking beast that sat low down on the drive itching to pounce for the open road and roar away at high speed. Barry came to the door looking like the country gent' that he tried to be, corduroy trousers check shirt a cravat and a waistcoat, but he didn't quite fit the role that he tried to portray.

Mrs Wright the 2nd who Mari had hardly seen and did not know her name was right behind him, curious to know what this little lady dressed in an oversized jumper and wellington boots wanted. She was dressed in a very short skirt, too short for the lady of the house. Her hair was raven black to match the overdone smudged eye-make-up and her jumper was the tightest possible thing on her skinny frame. She was thin to say the least. If Mari wanted to guess, she seemed to have had an afternoon session with the gin, but she was not here to judge, she was here to confront the man of the house. He realised that she was a woman on a mission. As she dropped herself to the ground from the Jeep, she was followed naturally by Brutus who was always by her side.

Then it happened...unexpectedly they came without warning, two of the biggest dogs they'd ever seen and attacked without a sound, until she heard Brutus squeal in fright and surprise. Mari had just approached Barry to say hello and extended her hand in greeting, just as Brutus emerged from the jeep.

But the terrible twosome were there to kill any intruder and Brutus was on their patch. It didn't take long to see the scene develop into a blood bath. Brutus didn't stand a chance the baring teeth cut into his throat and legs, the sound of a crack and then more of a 'help me' cry, but it was too late, he was almost dead. What a trap.

The cross bred boxer's left hook had caught him in his face followed by the amber beast, an Alsatian twice Bruno's size which looked somewhat like a lion. He had locked his teeth around his chest. They were there to kill, and the gentle Brutus was no match, it was an unfair contest.

Mari tried to pull them off but to no avail she too was attacked and mauled, the battle was over in a trice and ended with a shrill whistle that came from the back yard, the dogs backed off and scurried off with their tails between their legs, through the small side gate from where they came. It was not their fault that they were bred to kill, but it was over for Brutus.

Barry was mortified, the dogs were loose in the back yard but the side gate had been left partly open. He screamed to his wife to get out of the way and stay inside, then rushed to see to Mari who was by now lying protectively across her faithful Brutus. The blood spurted from the dog's throat and mouth and he was shaking in a fit like state, he was dying. Her arm was covered in blood, his and hers mingled in a torrent of red, but she managed to run to the back of the Jeep and get a blanket.

"Phone the vet, now" she demanded "Now". Panic took over and common sense left her, she should have known that Brutus was dead, but still she clung on to him.

"Too late", Barry said as he side stepped her to get to the dog making sure that he didn't soil his trousers as he did so. Blood doesn't come off that easily.

"Leave him", she shouted angrily "Just phone Greg tell him that your dogs have killed Brutus"

"An accident my dear Mari, a pure accident, you were on my land and they did what they had to do... PROTECT". He didn't care for her feelings it seemed.

Nothing more was said; it was only a dog.

She was too upset to pick an argument, and so just picked up her precious friend and placed him gently in the car, the blood seeped out through the back door like a leaky tap; it was both hers and his. Greg was at the gate when she arrived, tears streamed down her cheeks, and blood covered her thick jumper, she cried uncontrollably and just made it to the yard before she dropped to the ground and fainted. By some luck, Elsa the young cleaner was there to take her in and to peel her clothes off and clean her injuries, but Mari could not control the crying, that was mixed with anger as she tried to tell them what had happened.

The doctor was on his way, but Elsa as she bound her wounds with a fresh pillow case knew that she required more than a doctor...stitches, "I'm afraid so Miss Williams" said the doctor, "get in the car and I'll drive you down to the cottage hospital, no arguments".

The dog was taken away, Greg picked him up out from the back of the jeep and away from the bloody scene but Mari still wanted to see him one last time. But, there was no time. The doctor said that they shouldn't delay as she had lost a lot of blood, and things like that could wait a while. Then she was whisked down the lane with Elsa and the doc.

Brutus was lying on his blanket under the apple tree in the orchard, his favourite place to lie out of the hot sun today this was his last resting place. Max looked on and cried and would not leave, he rested his head on Brutus and tried to revive him. His best friend was gone.

There was no call from Barry.

Later that day Mari returned from the cottage hospital bandaged and splinted. She had a heavy cast on her right arm and her right thigh was stitched in a most awkward place close to the artery. She had been the luckiest woman alive it seemed, and she would be out of action for some time, but how will she recover from her old pal's death who was now buried in the orchard. Only she knew how she would do that.

Maybe Greg should have consulted her before making his own mind up where the old dog was to rest but he had to make the decision and that was it.

Mari did not ask about the dog until later that evening, and wanted to know whether he was wrapped in his favourite shawl. Greg assured her that he had done everything possible as the mangled body could easily be dug up by foxes. Then she walked quietly into the orchard alone. It was a moving moment. Greg stood back and left her alone and waited, was there going to be a cry, a whimper or just signs of despair ... Mari cried for many days. Greg was tearful but he must remain strong for Mari, this dog had seen her through some good and bad times.

Twelve years of companionship. A stray dog that once walked down the lane, lame and exhausted, obviously escaped from some brutal life and was seeking sanctuary and food. He had stayed close to her, protected her, expected nothing more than love in return.

Mari was bound to find the odd stray or two, likewise with Max found after a hit and run and gasping for breath as he crawled out of the undergrowth straight into her path, and only through pure luck and Brutus's bark did she veer away from where he was, then on quick examination and a trip to the vet's he was declared hers. A gift on a miserable rainy day. Then of course there's Greg, another stray of the human kind, there to stay forever it seems.

She walked slowly back from the grave, and simply said.

"This is not the end Greg, every dog has his day, and Brutus' day will come".

24 WINTER

It was a bitterly cold winter, the snow lay thick on the ground, stretching its fingers over the bushes and reaching beyond the tops of the stone walls. The road leading up to 'Y Graig' was impassable, and beyond that was Barry's place 'Rhandir Mwyn'. They were totally disconnected, marooned by the white stuff, but by some luck and common-sense Greg and Mari had been to the supermarket and filled the large freezer. Milk was provided by the cows and butter in abundance, bread was made weekly by Mari, and there was always some cakes or other delicacies. Potatoes were stored in the shed along with carrots and turnips, fresh eggs were laid daily by the chickens, there was always some meat but Greg had influenced Mari to become a vegetarian, but still favoured salmon and trout.

They would be fine.

Greg took this opportunity to draw and paint, as Mari had bought him some oils and canvas for Christmas. She carried on with her quilt, that had been set aside for years, and now with Greg as her extra pair of hands she had less to do on the farm; all was well and cosy in 'Y Graig'.

25 BARRY STUCK AND IN TROUBLE

The phone rang late one evening, Greg answered. It was a call for help from Barry. Rose, his young daughter, had been taken ill. Burst appendix they thought, and the ambulance couldn't get through because of the drifts and more snow was forecast on the way. They had suggested that they tried to get half way down the road and the snow plough might meet then part way to clear the rest of the narrow road, but it was impossible for any ambulance to get through.

As they set off to the hospital in the land Cruiser Barry was convinced that he could get through with his massive truck just like the one in the advert and what the salesman had told him he could do. But they got stuck in the stream that ran alongside the road. He hadn't seen it and had veered into the side and out of sight almost, the road and the hedgerows were level with each other, packed with snow. There were no visible land marks to denote which was the edge, or which was the hedge. So much for his big land cruiser thought Mari.

His voice became faint drifting through the blizzard then a whisper. "These new-fangled mobile phones, good for nothing and where do you put them, they're too big to go in your pocket"

"You can please yourself Greg, but you won't get me out there to help him, I will stay here and wait for your call, you will go with the tractor won't you?, take a blanket for the girl, but don't take Max".

The truck was lying in the snow almost face down and Rose looked almost dead in the passenger seat. The tractor would be too cold and open to take her all the way to the cottage hospital, so the only thing to do was to go back to Barry's place Rhandir Mwyn as there was no chance of turning the tractor round other than their entrance, but then he needed to get her to the hospital and fast.

After a long struggle and finding a gap to turn Greg returned to tow the big truck out if he could, but even for a strong tractor the truck was stubbornly wedged in the stream and the thick snow. Then there was the sound of another vehicle in the distance, and Mari appeared around the bend with the old jeep and its designer chains locked securely on the wheels, Mari knew about the winters here in Wales experience taught her to be prepared.

"Thought you wouldn't make it young 'un" and turned away from Barry. She was here to help Greg.

She carefully drove passed the truck and the tractor, just missing the wall on the other side of the narrow road and returned moments later.

"I'll tow and you push with the tractor Greg, we'll have them out in no time." She did not look at Barry but said that she hoped they were not too late. Rose tried to smile a thank-you. Then as if she was the master of her trade, she hitched the rope on to the land cruiser while the men looked on in awe of her strength and determination. Barry steered the big truck while Mari towed and Greg pushed as planned with the tractor. With all the power they all had they freed the truck that cruised no more, and as if it never happened Mari moved forward then unhitched the rope and turned into her own lane, Barry inched his way downhill to the main road followed by Greg in the old tractor just to make sure they were safe. There was a dent in the back of the heavy weight cruiser, and a dent in Barry's oversized pride she supposed, a costly business and Mari chuckled. There was no glimmer of gratitude from Barry, just a low thanks from Rose as she huddled into the blanket. They made it to the hospital in time to operate as she was fading fast. One minute longer and she would not have made it. There was no phone call from Barry, no thanks, but a column appeared in the daily newspaper.

26 "MAN CAUGHT IN SNOWDRIFT"

They had a tough time, the truck slipped and drifted through mountains of snow as they made their way down from the farm helped by Greg who pushed them out of the ditch with his tractor, and only for his own skilful driving and trying to console his brave young daughter Rose at the same time who was suffering with burst appendix, then they made it through.

He (Barry) had manoeuvred his truck skilfully back onto the road and brought his little girl to the hospital just in time.

There was no mention of Mari who did most of the work.

Greg was livid and spoiling for a fight, but just as calmly as before Mari patted him on the shoulder and said "Remember Brutus".

27 SPRING

Brutus's grave was covered with a fresh layer of fresh green grass, and the snowdrops were just peeking through the last of the winter snow. Soon the daffodils will show the way to spring. They will come out in bunches of yellow waiting for the bouquets of pinks and purple crocus to be delivered, the leaves on the apple trees will shine almost bright green in the sunlight waiting for the first apple to appear, then to dance over the old dog's resting place while Max will lay there guarding his bed.

Mari reckoned that the thick blanket of snow had kept Brutus warm through the winter, now the flowers would soon take over the task and bloom to keep him cool. She planted a few primroses; the delicate perfume would reach his nose so that he could sniff the air, and live in peace over the rainbow.

On some days Mari and Greg would stand there and look up to the sky and see the patterns in the clouds, sometimes they could see him there clearly running towards them and go again on the crest of another cloud. That is when Mari reckoned, he was happy and contented, he had his own pals. She knew he was happy, and she had her sweet memories of her big dog.

28 GILBERT

Then one bright day in the spring, a young lad came to the door fresh from college, enquiring about hiring the kiln room for the summer, he said. He knew that it was redundant and as yet there had been no decisions made on it. He had passed through with the school children last summer and had looked in, and as if by some quirk of fate, he had seen the advert in the local post office, with ideas to reopen the pottery shop.

He lived in the village and would like to start a pottery class but kilns were expensive and a readymade one was just the thing to get him started. He was also interested in the knitting room and wondered if that was free too. His sister Kate was a good knitter but could not afford a knitting machine or the facilities that Mari had.

Interesting! Mari thought, so the advert in the local paper and post office had paid off, although the ad' did not say that the premises were for rent, it was just a casually drawn picture of a knitting room showing their ideas for the future. A small cottage industry where people could walk and talk watch and learn.

The young lad's name was Gilbert Pritchard and wrote it on a piece of paper with his address and a telephone number to contact, then left in the hope of a favourable decision. Greg and Mari would mull it over and get back to him soon; they will check him out on their next visit to the village. Interesting! Thought Greg and he seemed a genuine young lad.

This was their first proper season and the cottages were fully booked, the idea of the kiln would be interesting for the visitors, and with his sister Kate taking over the knitting room alongside him it could work. So, they took a chance on Gilbert and Kate. They said that they had recently moved into the village with their parents. Mother was a secretary to a local solicitor and father was an estate agent, they wanted to give the children a chance to start their own business, and with the small amount of money they had saved Gilbert and Kate were both keen to go it alone and try their hand at being self-employed.

The road from the town on the other side of the hill was tidied and fit for cars to drive up to the farm. A new sign replaced the almost hidden half-forgotten one and a neat white sign that Greg had designed fitted perfectly beneath. The drive on the other side of the hill was also cleared and fit for purpose but not so much to spoil the rustic look of the place.

They had not bargained on such interest, Greg's Jerky Jenny was converted into a studio showing off his art work and the stable loft over the barn was converted into his work studio...perfect. He even had enquiries from schools and colleges to teach, and he was becoming well known and respected as an artist.

Mari's tea-pots were put to good use too, and with Elsa alongside her they turned the garden and orchard into a small tea-room, on sunny days.

Weeks turned into months and another year passed.

Barry still played his game of camping and a few caravans appeared, there was a toilet block built for convenience closer to his own yard. But it was noisy on the top field at times, he even held a festival one summer which went on for days and when the police were called Barry blamed Mari for being intolerant, but as he didn't have a licence to play music or sell liquor, he was heavily fined. They held barbecues that went on till dawn and their rubbish was strewn over the field, as Barry had not provided adequate bins that were always overflowing. His so-called visitors still came over the wall for teas and coffee and to take a look around Mari's place and to walk into the lovely forest on her land.

It seemed that Barry was still keen to be part of the action despite Mari's efforts to build and then to rebuild the walls, they still came through even though a wire fence was placed to try to deter them. Then one summer the police came round to talk to Mari about the barbed wire, one of the visitor's dogs had caught his leg on the barb and was bleeding badly, he had to go to the vet and they were charging her for the fees as Mr Barry Wright had suggested that the wires snared the dog and caused the deep gash.

There was no use protesting it seemed, as the dog was on Barry's side of the fence and was not trespassing when it was snared, he had dragged the already cut wire to free him-self and so ripped his leg open...but who had cut the wire and let the dog onto the field? Barry won again, sometimes she wondered if it had been deliberately cut and was all this worth it. Should she sell the top field to Barry, but then would he want more of her land? So, she still repeated over in her head. 'Remember Brutus every dog has his day' and then dismissed the idea of giving in again for a while.

People came from afar to see and stay at the farm, Sarah started giving riding lessons showing the children how to take care of the horses and taking rides out in the forest. Kate worked hard to get her knitting sessions going, and Mari's own knitting sold to the main store in town. Gilbert was the bees-knees with his young students' mainly young girls that swooned when he was near, they were learning to make pots jugs bowls and vases, but mainly because Gilbert was very handsome and each and every one thought they were his favourite so naturally he played to his audience.

Things were looking good for them all at the farm.

29 RUBBISH

One day when Greg went up to the road to collect the mail from the box, he noticed a black bag lying against the wall, and heard a dull whimper for help. He hesitated for one short moment and listened, then the black bag moved and he soon realised that there was a ...something in the bag, therefore he went forward to look inside. The bag whimpered and moved again right on cue as Greg cautiously opened it. The animal was trembling in fear and the cold that he had been subjected to throughout the night had left him numb.

Greg thought that he was a very young dog no more than two or maybe three years old, but that was only his assessment, on closer look when he arrived back at the house Mari took a good look, she thought that the gangly mutt was a cast out from greyhound racing, this dog had had his day it seemed and his use as a racing hound was over. His feet were bleeding and his neck was bruised blood red from an overtight collar or an attempt to strangle the poor thing.

How long had he been there, what could they do for this beautiful blue/black coloured dog, apart from feed him and take care of him for a while.

30 SOMETHING BLUE

After mulling it over and many names were considered Mari called him Blue, for now, although he was not there to stay of course and probably belonged to someone who cared, but who would toss him aside like that, unwanted with no collar no name, and so far from the main road.

He was not there to be found and just by luck he came to Mari's drive, so they must put a notice in the vet's surgery or the post office, the dog might be stolen from a good loving family and discarded by an unscrupulous thief. They will take him to the vet's on Monday to check him over. But Monday turned to Wednesday, and Blue was still there close to Mari and recovering from his ordeal.

Then on his way to the village Greg decided to take the task on and place the ad' in the vet's window 'lost and found' with details where to find him. Surely someone will know who owned the dog? But no one claimed him and so he became Mari's dog called Blue. He walked besides her everywhere; and he fed the chickens with Greg and watched as he milked the cows, looking forward to the warm cream poured into an old enamel dish that was a relic from Mari's home- made puddings.

Until one day, a few months later, a van came down the lane and a thin mean looking unkempt man stepped out, a part smoked cigarette dangled from his yellowed lips, his jacket smelled heavily of booze and his nose was running almost into his mouth, which he wiped with a dirty rag that he produced from his torn pocket. His unwashed hair was thin and wispy long and greasy, and he was bald on top, but reluctant to have a haircut as he had always had long hair in his youth…a blast from the past, a person that remained in a time warp, and had not noticed the changes as years passed him by.

There was a sick looking dog in the passenger seat gazing longingly to be allowed out, he was a greyhound that looked thinner than lean, the thin man and the sad dog was a miserable looking pair. The man slammed the door as the greyhound tried to make his move for clean air, but it was too late, the door slammed on his face, he yelped but was not noticed, and he backed away into his seat in despair.

The man walked lazily towards the house where Mari stood, and on seeing him, Blue backed off and tried to make it to the house, but on command of "Come 'ere" from the mean man the dog froze and shivered.

"My dog you got there missus, I've come to collect or you must pay for him, where did you find him? He escaped from the pen one night and we've been looking for him"

That's a lie Mari thought, he couldn't give a damn about the dog and money was the only thing on his mind, how much could he get for this once poor neglected dog that was now a beautiful Blue lean machine.

Greg was close to the wreck on wheels, a limping van that could do with a new set of tyres, Greg thought, as he remembered his worn tyres. He was scrutinizing the contents through the window. The back of the van was a shamble, an old tyre, a can of dirty looking oil, an oily rag, a thick rope and some wire netting were inside. It was a death trap on wheels, one lighted match would have done it and there was a small mongrel with a look of despair huddled amongst it all. The greyhound in the front was wining to be set free, and discretely Greg opened the door to let him out, he too was limping badly and had whip marks across his back. He ran as far as he could from the mean man who had carelessly thrown his fag end on the ground and was half-heartedly running after the lame dog, but suddenly Max was on the defence as Mari seemed to be in the way of the man that was heading straight for her to retrieve his dog.

Max was having none of it and threw himself across his path...he fell backwards of course, and tried to defend himself from these fierce animals. Max and Blue were poised menacingly over him but did not harm him, even though he had kicked them hard and swore at the Blue one.

Greg walked towards them with the tiny skinny puppy in his arms.

"And how much do you want for the lot then?".

But the man wanted to escape; he was outnumbered by people and dogs.

He stuttered "Te...wenty quid will do it, or M..y-be another ten for the old 'un.

Greg went in for some cash and a piece of paper which served as a receipt, and asked the lean smelly man to scribble his name at the bottom of the page for the sale of the dogs. Then he was off down the road as fast as his old banger would go, stuffing the cash into his torn pocket, and lighting one fag from the other... the death trap on wheels was ready to explode.

"Close the gate behind you," Mari called out, "we don't want any more scoundrels around here".

They phoned the police later that day, who knew about the guy that had already been prosecuted for the same offence; breeding and selling, and if and when the dogs were too old to sell then they were dumped. They would detain him forthwith and notify the authorities of his activities, and assured Greg that he will not get away with it. Now they had three extra dogs, Brutus will be glad of the company. But the puppy found his place underneath Gilbert's chair and slept soundly to the rhythm of the potter's wheel as Gilbert worked his magic to create another masterpiece, a jug to match another set or a goblet to go with the other dozen. So, he was adopted by him and Kate, and called Pee-wee for obvious reasons being a very nervous pup. The oldest and biggest was known as Fred, he had that old-fashioned look of a greyhound, a know all about the racing world, with his flat (Andy cap) cap look about him. An old racing greyhound well past his best. He lolloped around and snoozed and snored loudly under the old apple tree with Blue, just like two old men discussing the day's events.

31 ELSA

Elsa moved into the house that summer. There had been a spot of bother at home, and as she was the eldest one of four children she decided to leave, but where would she go? She did want to keep her job with Mari and Greg. Neither Greg nor Mari suspected that there was anything wrong at home, until the happy girl revealed that her step-father had more than a fatherly interest in her. At times he had tried his hand to be more than friendly. At first she 'did not tell' but when the situation became worse and she had managed to avoid the inevitable outcome she knew that he would not leave her alone. On the second and third attempt she became frightened, and so as not to upset her mother made her decision to go, perhaps it was better that way.

So, she confided in Mari who told Greg, and with one swoop of her belongings into the Jeep she had her own bedroom that looked out over the orchard at the back of the house. She was sorry for her mother of course...who suspected nothing.

32 SPRINGS TURNED INTO SUMMERS

Business was booming at the farm throughout the seasons. The peace and quiet and the cool winds of autumn brought a welcome relief, the cooler wintery weather would be a welcome change. Big shot Barry had been the same nuisance with what he called festivals that went on till day break. Mari feared for the visitors in the cottages, some quiet reserved people that had come away for a break, but nobody complained, so far. He was still pushing down the walls from his field to hers to let his people pass through to walk in the forest, some undesirable characters that did not give a damn about the wildlife and livestock in the fields.

So, in the Autumn there was work to be done, walls to re-build and a fresh coat of paint in and out of the cottages. The house could do with a new look too, so Gilbert lent a hand with all the chores, and even Kate made some new covers for the beds, while Elsa and Mari prepared for the bad weather to come.

"Team work that's what it is" Mari said.

Gilbert was showing a lot of interest in Elsa, who was about twenty-six years old by now, quiet, reserved and shy but funny when she was with the people she knew. There was a glint in his eye, and he was always keen to give her a helping hand with everything she did. So it seemed that dear Gilbert was there to lend more than a helping hand... he was there for Elsa; although Elsa showed no interest in him, after all she had bad memories of men that wanted to touch her.

33 OCTOBER

Greg's birthday was close to Mari's birthday in dates, she would be sixty-nine (he suspected) and he would be thirty in October. One week later. He had been there for ten years in this place he called home. 'My goodness how time flies', and this had become his life, the farm, the changes the work, and dear Mari who had become his mum, it was all worth it just to see her smile, and she always smiled. Elsa, Kate and Gilbert decided to throw a party for them both at the farm; the end of the season was a good time when people could relax a bit and then continue with their work refreshed and ready to go. After all their family had grown from two to five already not forgetting dear Sarah that bobbed in from time to time, especially if she had tales from the outside world to tell.

She lived with her mother on the other side of the hill. Her mother was a solicitor and had had some dealings with Barry who had caused a bit of a nuisance in the town. He was bolshie and thought that he was untouchable in his big red car, so when he was brought in for drinking and disturbing the peace, he elected Sarah's mother to defend him on a couple of issues.

Sarah had to pass by Barry's house before she reached Mari's place 'Y Graig'.

He approached her one day and offered her a good deal... the use of his barns and stable block for nothing; in fact, he offered to advertise her little venture of riding lessons, and said that his road and yard was much better for cars and land Rovers to drive in than Mari's place. No rutty road to manoeuvre and lots more space to park. Strange offer she thought, and what did he want in exchange? Some information about what was happening at the farm, was Mari ready to sell?

But when she declined his offer, he was like a person scorned, and didn't take too kindly to being refused, especially when it was such a good deal, and he drove back down the drive like a maniac on his brand-new glossy quad- bike. So, Sarah came back with the news and thought that he was up to no good. Her mother would not defend him again.

34 THE PARTY

They would invite all the neighbours from the village to the party, and business people would come and see what they were up to. They might tell them about another three conversions they had planned; the old ruined pig sty and coal shed had been marked out for cottages. But what could Greg buy Mari for her birthday?

This was his dilemma as he had never bought anyone a special gift before, besides she was from another generation and she had most things it seemed. She needed nothing in her plain and simple life. She didn't even realise that her farm was on the map as a holiday spot. Should he paint a picture? Oil on canvas was his favourite. Should he confer with the others and they could buy something together? No. This gift would be especially from him and him alone.

But what was Mari planning? Was she thinking of his birthday too?

Unbeknown to him, the famous four , Elsa, Kate, Sarah and Gilbert were planning this party and more, and would combine both his with Mari's surprise on the same day good idea but the plot thickens, what could Mari give him as a birthday gift? A dilemma, as Greg was quite contented with his life and needed nothing, especially now that Mari had bought him a new jeep... (Well, nearly new).

So, what could she get him?

She had her ideas tucked away in one of the bigger tea-pots, her secret and her rainy-day pot, and with a little help from her friends she could pull it off. Greg plotted too and with very little time and no way to hide his surprise he worked on his painting in secret only revealed to Elsa, the only one that would not tell. But Elsa and Gilbert were keeping Mari's bigger secret surprise too. He would never guess in a million years.

The painting was almost done.

It was what Greg always wanted to draw and paint, and hoped that she would like it.

First, he sketched her at work in the kitchen, kneading the dough methodically and looking up at him smiling as she always did. As far as she was concerned this was just another of his scribbles that would be put away and forgotten like many others until he got 'round to painting it. There was old Blue the dog sleeping under the table, and her rocking chair that seemed to be rocking to and fro to the motion of the kneading and pummelling of the dough. There were trays laid out on the table ready for cakes and the old notched wooden rolling pin set aside, almost there as a reminder to get her a new one, but then she would still use the old one no doubt, the one that had seen years of rolling over and over.

Each day and with every changed movement he sketched until he was satisfied and ready to paint then frame the finished oil painting to present to her on her birthday.

Elsa was always on hand ready to steer her away from his work room with an excuse that would keep her occupied for a while. But then again, she didn't go up those dangerous steps very much these days. Of course, there was Mari's surprise, poor Elsa who was keeping that secret away from Greg. The numerous trips into town, to arrange his Art Exhibition without arousing suspicion was a task on its own. Leaflets and invitations sent out all over the country to view this little-known artist's work, of course they could not have done it alone. Kate skilfully put the package together and had managed to work from home to advertise and use her mother's computer, and as Greg had no such thing as a computer that secret presented little or no problem.

But there was a problem, and that was to get his paintings out of his work-shop and into the Jeep the day before the exhibition, as Greg knew every drawing and painting, every nook and cranny every pen and pencil. It would be awkward. Therefore Gilbert was volunteered to take him to London to another art exhibition...tricky but it could be done.

Early start and late return should solve the problem.

So, they were put safely on the train and away from the problem.

This is where he confided in Gilbert about his painting called 'Woman at Work' and he told him of his plan that was to place it in the kitchen before she woke up in the morning. But Gilbert knew about the painting, Elsa had not been able to keep it to herself, and besides she needed his help to pull the whole thing off, and who better to trust than dear besotted loved up Gilbert.

35 THOUGHTS AND SCHEMES

But Gilbert had another idea! What about putting it in the exhibition with the others, but how without anyone suspecting? Simple that's how. He would tell Greg that he would hide it, then she would find it later in the day, and so Greg accepted his idea but told him to be very careful as it had taken him many hours and days to paint. They enjoyed their day in the city, two buddies enjoying the day out. Greg loved and looked at the paintings over and over again, "I'd love to have mine in an exhibition like this, but then mine are just amateur drawings"

Gilbert was more interested in the sculpture.

"Same here" Gilbert said "but maybe one day Eh!"

They had a few pints in a bar close to the river, and watched the day come to an end and had a meal in a nearby pub. Greg sketched a bit; things around him intrigued him, small boats with banners and balloons chugging away on the Thames with young people enjoying their parties, and girls in tight Lycra pants jogging past. A taxi driver arguing with his customer, and a child pulled along by its mother, hurrying to the tube station. It was so different from his world up in the hills of Wales. He thought that he would like to come again and take a closer look.

A couple stopped by their table and looked over his shoulder, amazed at the speed and the dexterity of his drawing, an art in itself learnt over the years of street painting, the more he drew the more money he made, and then he could eat. Then, another one leaned over it was almost like old times,

"You should be in one of them exhibitions", the guy said with an American accent.

"One day he'll make it" Gilbert said quietly, and chuckled.

"Is London the place for you Greg, if you ever made it big and you had to live here, or is your heart set in Wales now"

Greg did not answer, he had enjoyed his day, and they were going home. They arrived back at the station tired; Kate was there to meet them she seemed tired; she'd had a long day too. The day's events of pulling and pushing, carrying and hanging the paintings, while Sarah and her mother helped to place them in order of dates and times. There had been a lot of organizing for this his big day.

From here Greg would drive himself up to the farm, and let them go home. It was a dark night, and all of a sudden a very expensive looking sports car came hurtling 'round the bend.

"What the hell" thought Greg swerving out of the way, "some-one in a hurry, a woman driver no doubt, but so late and here on the lane"?

He mentioned it to Mari, who was on her way to bed; she too looked tired and did not listen, she was usually keen to hear what he had to say but not tonight, what was going on?

36 THE DAY OF THE EXHIBITION

Greg was up early to talk to Gilbert about his painting and where to hide it as a surprise for Mari, but Gilbert was nowhere to be seen. Now Greg was concerned, the key to his work shop would not turn no way could he make it open, the cows needed milking the goats and the rest of the animals had to be fed, so his painting in the work shop would wait. Mari and Elsa were impatiently waiting to go into town to celebrate Mari's birthday at a new restaurant that had opened or so Greg thought, and it seemed that Gilbert would meet them there. He'd left it a bit late to come up to the farm, slept in after their tiring day yesterday...

Strange thought Greg, he'd promised to find a good place to hide Mari's surprise painting.

No doubt he will explain when he makes his appearance. He would never let him down at a time like this.

Mari looked lovely, Kate had done her hair and make-up 'specially for the do, and they had obviously had time to shop as she had new shoes and a neat dress. There was a new shirt ready pressed for Greg and a pair of new jeans, so this was going to be a special do then, he hadn't had a new shirt in ages and it fitted perfectly.

'But just you wait Gilbert, you'll get a piece of my mind...now where would he have put my painting'? Just then a posh Limo' pulled up in the yard, what the hell was it all about??? Mari's birthday wasn't that such a big deal, surely?

But it wasn't all for Mari.

A new restaurant eh! Not in the town hall? But there they were pulling up close to the car that had almost driven him off the road late last night. There were many more cars in the usually empty car park, and a camper van and trailer with...

'The Vagabonds' written on the side in Blue sign writing against the glowing silver camper, an advert for one of the up and coming folk groups touring Britain and beyond, a group he had vaguely heard of but had not had the time to listen to carefully, but the guitar and vocal seemed familiar and as he was ushered up the steps and through the main door, he knew why.

A band called The Vagabonds stood to the side of another door that led into the main hall. His best mates that he had left behind. Mel and Ross smartly dressed singing a song he knew. One that Ross had written to match Greg's art work as he painted alongside them. There were two others in the band, a long-haired drummer and a key board player. What the hell was happening, and how did they find them? Greg was in shock, and went forward to greet them almost falling over a framed painting of Brutus leaping up in the air to reach for the sky, clouds of white and shadows as he made his way up and away.

"Missed you last night, didn't I?" Mel said "I was in a rush to get this ready for today, good eh! You've come a long way from the streets Greg"

And so had they, but there was more.

"See you later up at the ranch now go and see what else you've done that you had forgotten about"

The first thing that greeted him was the extravagant looking board, announcing Greg: The unknown artist.

And the painting of Mari right there in front of them.

Mari was in tears, and could not go on, Gilbert said that it was a gift from Greg.

The sly old bugger he had it there all this time, no wonder he couldn't get into his work shop.

The next drawing was of a boy walking down the dark road head down and paint brushes in his hand, that was one of his earliest drawings in pencil and charcoal but it was pretty good he thought. Many other paintings and drawings were exhibited and the very first of the cottage when he had arrived there that he eventually finished.

There was the gate hanging off its hinges and another of the same gate drawn in charcoal repaired and swinging happily in the breeze, crooked walls with big boulders that were the strong base to steady the whole thing, graduating to smaller rocks and stones. Painting of long tracks through the dense forest where foxes, rabbits and any other creatures made their way safely home to their burrows and dens, looking furtively over their shoulders for that ... a just in case moment of distraction, a pounce, and death.

So many he had painted and drawn set aside for another day he thought, and how were they able to put it all together for this exhibition he never suspected for one moment and had not noticed that they were gone? But there was one strange and roughly drawn in pencil.

A beef burger van, with Barry serving tea and making a sausage sandwich, it was a humorous drawing, with the sausages falling out of the pan and a make believe dog waiting to steal whatever he could reach, and in addition...in the corner a rough sketch of a police car in the distance, watching and waiting it was all a made up scene of course, but this drawing that had a 'Sold' tag on it already.

'Who the hell would want that' he considered. Barry was a bit of a cartoon figure in the drawing, with his red braces hanging down on to his hips. His name up in lights in red greens and yellow over the canopy. Greg had not realized at the time, that he would get to know Barry so well. But it was all done with a smile and good humour, or so he thought.

But there was more:

37 THE PARTY

Later that day there was a party;
 Many friends and business people who were keen to see what their next venture was at the farm, and they were all there to give their in-put and advice.

Gilbert showed them 'round the place, his Kiln room and all the plates and various things he had made, The postmistress was keen to give him a section in her shop in town to display his wares. She had ideas on extending her little shop into the yard at the back. Kate's knitting shed went down well with a lady that wanted to buy some of her fine sweaters for her high-end designer shop in London...they would be in touch.

Greg of course could not get enough of his pals Mel and Ross, who had come to the decision to clean up their act after Greg left. They were no longer a threesome and it was getting quite dangerous on the streets. They had no transport or a mattress to sleep on and so as time went by, they made their way into clubs and pubs, eventually noticed by another couple who lived in Chelsea who had their own recording studio. They moved in with them and Ross was thrilled to have his own space to play and write his own songs for Mel and the group to sing.

They made it slowly up the charts and now were in business, "Hence the new car. I always wanted a sporty number, but not knowing these country roads I just missed you last night, I would have been upset if I had ruined my car, not forgetting that I might have injured you too" she still had that sense of humour she had back then.

They were married now her and Ross, "Two children, four and two, still waiting for their god-father to turn up to have them christened, so how's about it come up to London and do some work with us, stay awhile and paint"?

The invitation was tempting: to be with his old pals for a couple of weeks, a chance to paint different things. The Thames, the old London streets, the docks and even to watch other buskers and pavement artists at work. Younger ones now of course with a different look at life. Yes, it would be nice to stay awhile, meet other likeminded people and even ones he had never met. He would go, especially as he was to be the children's godfather.

"We will arrange to have the children blessed" Ross said

"You cannot turn us down for that, can you?"

So, promises were made for an early spring date, and a short stay with them.

Greg likewise said that they were welcome to stay here in the summer, but it seemed that they had a tight schedule for the coming year and would check with their agent.

'Agent eh! My goodness they have made it, and there was he worried that he had let them down'

They stayed overnight in one of the new cottages but had to leave the next day...children, and work was the order of the day. After exchanging notes and phone numbers, they asked if they could have one of the old drawings printed for the cover of their new Album called 'Escape' and Greg was pleased to sign the original as 'One of us', with a scribble that was his signature.

38 PROMISES

Mari was curious to know what had been said.

"I think they want you to go to London, don't they? It might be a good idea, they say that the streets are paved with gold, Greg, but I never found any nuggets when I was there, get out and about a bit see the sights again, there are lots to see."

Mari didn't mean it, she would miss him but she did remember her time in London and the bright lights that had blinded her, and she could tell that he was drawn to be with his friends again, days passed and he hadn't thought too much about their invitation so it was dismissed for now.

Monday morning, and the phone didn't stop ringing. Could they come up and see his paintings. Another request was for the gates painting. And the painting of the woman with the flour on her cheeks was it For Sale? By Monday afternoon, Greg's book was full of enquiries. Talks and exhibition requests were flooding in. But who had reserved the drawing of the beef-burger van, and what a silly quick drawing it was? Mind you...it was funny. His answer came in a flash of a red Ferrari, whooshing its way into the yard. It was Barry.

"Come for me paintin' and I want you to sign it". There was no please, or thanks.

Of course, it was Barry who else would it have been, his curiosity had got the better of him and had made it to the art exhibition before anyone else. Greg was not about to sign or sell for that matter, not yet anyway, but here was one proviso.

"I'll sell it to you on one condition, and that is that you don't try to sell it on, no profit and no loss, but it's unsigned as I am an unknown artist, it won't be worth much"

Greg was not about to put his name to anything that had to do with Barry, besides he could have it forged, and who knew better than Greg about forgery? He could have made a lot of money...once upon a time long, long ago.

"Didn't know you could draw youngster? But that aint 'alf bad"

"Do you still want it Barry, I'll have it ready by tomorrow, twelve noon should do it, would you like me to tidy it up a bit leave it in the frame or not, the cost with the frame is seventy quid, friends terms but you must not sell it on, it will be priceless one day...maybe?

Barry agreed the price and the terms, and handed Greg the cash from his thick wad, both were happy, CASH DEAL NO QUESTIONS ASKED.

The days were full of surprises.

Greg worked in his work-shop that day putting the paintings back where they belonged in tidy heaps this time, and yet again more of his old paintings and drawings were found. Some were just sketchings on rough paper and could be re-done some even printed, but refreshed and worked on. All these would be quite something, although a daunting task, remembering things that he didn't want to remember but there was great depth and feeling to some of them and with his expertise... Bring them to life; they were as rough as the paper he had drawn on as a teenager, and original of course.

He sat for a while pondering remembering his past. Grandad and that one photo of himself and his mother, and he cried for the first time in years.

He had no desire to go back to his past other than forward to meet his pals and taste the city life where they belonged, so life was turning almost full circle and strangely he looked forward to being with them again, besides he needed to work on the logo on their posh trailer, spruce it up a bit.

In the meantime, Barry came to collect his drawing, still framed as he requested.

A few words of thanks and a sideways glance at the new buildings and he was off roaring down the lane frightening the hell out of Sarah's horses...what a beast Greg thought, what an idiot, what a car, and he did not even get out to close the gate, but it did swing shut behind him, missing the Ferrari by an inch.

But Greg smiled to himself. The drawing was not the original, it was a print that he ran up early this morning, and there were three more waiting to be sold with a signature, it wasn't even the first of the three prints, so let's wait until he tries to sell it shall we? And he is bound to try and sell it. But Barry wouldn't know the difference anyway.

Months passed into another season;

March and it was beginning to feel warmer; the grass had grown over Brutus' grave. There was hardly a bump there now, and just a small slate attached to the tree with Beautiful Brutus written on it.

There were two new lambs bought for the children that visited to stroke and tickle, and the older ewes were getting fat. One of the older goats died and Jack the goat came in to replace him, a young thing that loved to follow Elsa around as he was sure of a carrot or two if he butted hard enough. That was their party piece and the children loved it. The chickens laid their golden eggs but yet again they were old hens and a couple had gone to pastures new, replaced with new chicks all yellow and fluffy ready for the coming season. All the animals on the farm were rescued from one bad situation or another and now were happy, Blue sat close to Mari listening to her singing melodious Welsh tunes.

There was always a large bundle of post in the box these days and sometimes if there was too much the postman would bring it down to the house, stay for a quick cup of tea and set off again. It was a good excuse to browse through Greg's paintings, as he was not a bad artist himself and would often show Greg his latest landscape then get his advice and tweaks if they needed improving, and they always needed that special touch from Greg.

He would tell them about things that were happening in the village, and the Fete and Festivals coming up in May, and hoped that Greg could donate one of his paintings to the fete. Mari would give some of her tea cosies, Gilbert to give a jug and Kate would donate a hat and scarf. Sarah was on hand with the small welsh pony, to give the children rides there and back round the green. It seemed that Barry had advertised his place for campers and caravans, showing the walks and views over to the forests from the top field.

"He wasn't popular with the villagers or the police last summer I'll tell ya, and one or two caused a bit of a scene in the 'The Red Dragon 'Chinese restaurant. They walked out without paying, said that their meals were cold, and one produced a nail from his curry. Now you and I know that Dear Ming is as clean and careful as can be, but they were there looking for trouble.

It turned out that he had a few similar nails in his pocket, and the situation was only defused when Barry (who didn't want any trouble) came on the scene, so they are keeping an eye on Barry's friends and movements...Always been a pain in the Ass has Barry, a bad lad from the day he came to the village ...a misfit with a bit of brass, and language to match. Whatever happened there with the old missus Wright is still a mystery, and then the old man himself. Sick one day and died the next.

Still they did the honourable thing and buried him with his wife in a grave on the farm a small patch in the orchard as he requested, lovely man the old John Wright (the graves are fenced off with a chain and padlock), and then this Barry boy and his mother, and now his wife and his daughter Rose. She's not bad, at least not as bad as her Dad, but you know what they say. The apple never falls far from the tree.

So, postman George was off on his way again, having gossiped a bit more. George knew more about somethings, after all he was postman and delivering news good or bad, it was part and parcel of his job.

"Close the gate; we don't want any ruffians coming by...Ta"

There was a large envelope addressed to Greg, an invitation to Chelsea and the christening of Mel and Ross' two children.

P.S "They will be going to school soon and still no God Father, come and do your duty".

So, he was to go to London in two weeks' time, and not he would not forget to take his brushes and charcoal, lots to see and paint, and maybe a portrait of the children! Maybe you'll stay!

Tall order he thought as he was only planning to stay the week-end.

Everyone at the farm was sorry to see him go, it wasn't as if he was going abroad to a far distant land but Mari was almost in tears and wondered if he would come back, but he had packed very little therefore she hoped that it was just for the week-end.

He left with Gilbert in a jolly mood and prepared for what was to come but a little sad to leave his pals and his home, but he must go as Mel and Ross were also his pals.

"Take care of the business" he said as he made his way across the bridge to the train "I'll be back on Tuesday".

39 LONDON

They were both there to meet him with two small children, Robert and Elizabeth, in tow and they greeted him with open arms and held his hand tightly.

It was a strange feeling, London. As if he was in a completely strange land. People were bustling to and fro to catch their train and meet friends and family, no time to stop for breath, and certainly not for chatting.

No one seemed to care about others and nobody noticed them as they made their way towards the Taxi Rank, but Greg did notice an advert for a concert to be held in a swank hotel in Knightsbridge with the famous 'Vagabonds' taking the top billing, a charity do with host of guests including Royalty.

The cover of their album, in the corner of the advert that was on the side of a bus with three buskers looking straight at him, one drawing one singing and a guitarist...impressive, but room for improvement round the edges he thought...could do better next time.

The taxi driver recognized the trio and wished them well for tomorrow night's do." Some event for you three then, good luck with the Royals".

Their small flat was lovely, compact and bijou as Mel had wished. A play room just big enough for the children, their toys and bunk beds. Two other bedrooms (small) and a small kitchen and lounge with a corner view of London and the ever honking of horns and unfamiliar sounds.

No goats and no barking dogs, no Mari's whistle for breakfast.

Mel showed him his room that had no view other than a back street with bins and rubbish strewn around, a narrow lane running on to the busy street and high-class shops, nothing glamourous about that then.

It was like everything happened; 'Front of house' and the back alleys were never on view. This was quite an exclusive part of town.

He was taken by surprise, there seemed to be a rush to go everywhere.

They were going down to the hotel for a final rehearsal this evening; where they would do some sound checks. There would be a gathering of some body guards, secretaries, minders and producers, a small audience to make them feel comfortable.

Greg was to go along and watch; besides they had to get him fitted for an evening suit for tomorrow.

Plans were already taking shape and he knew nothing about the special evening that was to take place; in fact, he was surprised that they were so in demand…Mel and Ross… Wow!

After the fitting, (which was paid for from the bank of the Vagabonds) and the rehearsal in the main room full of dignitaries, wires and cameras, he was carried on the crest of a wave from the rehearsal to a lovely little Italian restaurant in Soho, where they were served expensive pizzas. They watched the street artists that sat with their easels, drawing away as he did once and the buskers sang just as Mel and Ross had done but they were past that now, and he thought that the twosome was indifferent to what was once their struggle to survive.

Forgotten like a bad dream, and for him, it was streets away from Wales.

The following morning was the day of the christening, a small affair that started at eleven o' clock. Elizabeth came bounding into the room to show her new pink dress her mother had bought her, and Robert was there behind her in his little tuxedo a, cravat and patent shoes, just the thing for a little man going on a date. So it went from morning till it was time to run again, so off they went to this gig, and Royalty.

Tux on and hair straightened but tousled, Greg was not one for pomp and ceremony, and couldn't care less about Royalty he did have that careless good-looking Vagabond look about him, he looked more like a well-dressed Bob Geldof with the looks of Hugh Grant, than Greg the artist.

He was placed to sit on the front table close to the Prince and was made so welcome by the entourage that guarded him that he felt no pressure or nervousness, there was a smattering of pretty girls around to add to the décor, and Greg was quite a hit with one or two ladies that were made up to extreme, with their false eye lashes that fluttered his way, and boobs that fluttered over their low cut dresses, pleading you to look and check them out, and so he did.

It was a great night, and the band was good, they had another guitarist and a keyboard player, the sound around was superb, so professional so polished. And everyone enjoyed the show. The Vagabonds were about to take their bow at the end of the show and Mel thanked them for the donations that had come in for their chosen charity 'The homeless people in London', it had surpassed all expectations. So, she hadn't quite forgotten her past after-all.

"But" she went on in her professional way, well used to an audience by now, "Please let me introduce you to the last vagabond, Greg Mason the man that started it all. He gave us this big break and set us on the right road, otherwise we would still have been three Vagabonds trying to make it through life on the streets"

The lights panned on to Greg, and a standing ovation followed as Mel beckoned him up onto the stage.

Greg tried to flatten his unruly hair and shyly made his way next to Mel and Ross; once more she said "The Three Vagabonds" and more cheers followed.

He mingled with the Prince and his guests until it was time for the Royals to leave, but not before he asked Greg about his venture in Wales, He was keen to know about things that were going on in Wales.

"After all I am the Prince of Wales you know".

Obviously, someone had done some research on his behalf, but as it was past his bedtime and had a heavy schedule ahead, he asked Greg to hand his card to one of his secretaries and shook his hand once more to the flash of cameras. With that he was whisked into the waiting Rolls where a crowd had gathered to see him, and then he was gone with a smile and a wave of thanks.

'A very Royal do but was it me, has this just happened to me, Greg thought?'

What a tale he had to tell when he gets back home.

But he was in for another surprise the following day.

Ross and Mel had arranged to take him out to lunch but first they had an interview, someone was interested in a three-part documentary about how they met and their life before they met;

The beginning, the middle, and the rekindling of their friendship again or was it the end for the trio, or a beginning of a new life. A success story about three individuals that made it from street to stage, who knows, this could even make it as a film.

This is where Greg drew the line, he did not want to dwell on the past and he was sure that Ross didn't either as his life had been similar to Greg's but Mel was keen, she wanted to be someone, and this was another link to opportunity and a step closer to the top of the ladder.

Greg must have time to think... how did he get here anyway?

The christening was fine and that was what he was here for, and then he would be back home to deal with his own business, he was well out of his comfort zone in the city and he knew exactly where he belonged. They would give their answer in a couple of weeks, although they knew that it would be without him, but today was for sightseeing and lunch. There was one more stop before the day was over;

Down a narrow street, then through some doors into an Art Gallery.

This was something else, not like the one that was held in the village on his birthday, but this was the crème de la crème of the art world, from Monet to the most modern art. It was a quiet place where experts mingled with ones that just appreciated art and they wandered and studied the artist's work admiring the difficult forms, the intricacies, the clever way he or she had captured the light and shade in the painting, the abstract paintings that were so modern in contrast created by new artists.

There was the section for up and coming artists.

Smack on the middle wall was Greg's painting of Mari at work in the kitchen with the almost swaying rocking chair in a prominent position, he could see what he had created now as the lights reflected on Mari's face enhancing her rosy cheeks and her sincere smile that was quite natural.

And Brutus!

The Flying Dog?

Reaching high in the air his silhouette bold at first, against the clouds then fading to reach for the sky and beyond. The artist has captured the movement and the moment with great skill and consideration, was a short piece written on the gold bound leaflet that was handed to each of them as they entered.

"Interesting isn't it" commented a man who was studying the dog and its three disappearing shadows and the hand that reached out to him in the clouds enveloping him and taking him to safety.

Greg was speechless and Ross and Mel smiled.

"This is a gift for being godfather and friend, your own paintings in a famous gallery".

"But how did you get the paintings and who helped...did Mari know...and the rest of them?"

"They all knew and the paintings travelled with you on the train and delivered here last night, there has been some interest in both paintings if you want to sell"

"The rotten lot" he said I cannot trust any one of them" and laughed out loud then went back to the gentleman that was studying the dog.

"It's my painting, I painted that, and I am the artist" he said with pride.

"Then I shall buy it" said the distinguished gentleman "Name your price, my boy".

40 MONDAY MORNING

Mari sat quietly alone with her morning cup of tea, the first of the day. It was always the best.

Soon it would be time to feed the hungry brood, "And what about you Blue do you think that the boy will come back home, or will the lights of London dazzle him, his friends and now his friend The Prince, new and old friends that will make him famous. So, we must wait and see, eh?"

Greg treated Mel and Ross to dinner that night, a modest looking sort of place from the outside, but a grand fish 'n chip shop "Not quite like Louis' plaice".

They had champagne and beer, and then went back to the flat; Greg closed the curtains on the back alley and laid back on the pillow, it was a far cry from when they used to sleep in the VW, huddled together to keep warm during the winter. But the roar of the traffic and doors banging kept him awake here in the city, until eventually he dozed as he reflected on the past events and his week-end in London.

41 THE CITY WAS NOT FOR HIM

Mel and Ross knew that he wouldn't stay; he had made his life in Wales,
And what about Mari who would repair the gates and clear the lanes?
Greg would return.

There was a welcoming party waiting for him at the station, apart from Gilbert and Kate, there was Barry. He had tried to sell the original painting (that wasn't) and was there to confront him there and then.

"You've only gone and sold me a copy, you little squeak, so where is it, the original?"

Greg looked quizzically at the red-faced bully that stood against him pushing and thrusting himself till Greg was up against the wall.

"What the hell are you on about Barry? That is what you saw and that is what you bought, so you tell me that I sold you a copy? There are three copies then and no original 'cos I can't tell the difference either".

With one unexpected hard shove Barry landed on his back in the muddy puddle, Gilbert came hurrying forward with Pee Wee who threw him back again into the mud.

"By the way Barry, get your beef burger wagon cleaned up, the police will be calling to see you, nasty smell of weed around the van and it's not mint. I smelled it the first time I saw you and you don't smell so sweet yourself. It lingers around the face you know Barry, it's one smell I was used to once upon a time".

So that's how Barry made his money, the festivals and bad crowd where they delivered the goodies. Is that why he wanted access through the farm from the bottom road, straight off the main road and in easily over Mari's field onto his own?

"Watch your back Barry, someone will tell the cops one day, and it won't be me"

Later that season, the old dog Max died and so did the old greyhound, missing their walks together in the nearby forest perhaps! So, they took their place just there amongst the tall trees where they used to walk... and a new fir tree was planted to mark the spot. Greg missed his pal Max so much that he stopped painting for a while, even though people were asking for paintings of rickety old gates and wonky dogs.

Until; one day Elsa walked in with two, three-year-old, mature Alsatians, Betty and Ace. Ace was as black as coal with unusually pale blue eyes, watching, observing like a good detective, until it was time to pounce.

Betty was a pale almond almost white dog that looked like a wolf and could be seen miles away, she was almost a ghostly figure if you met her on a dark night when the moon was high and the wind howled.

"Now tell me if they are not welcome, I can take them back", said Elsa knowing full-well that they were there to stay.

"Betty didn't work out as a police dog, she was like a beacon that glowed and gave the game away, and Ace's handler has retired and the dog doesn't want to work anymore without him, the two dogs are big pals and would like to stay together"

Mari could not resist Ace, not that he looked like Brutus but there was a resemblance there. " Of course, he can stay", and he immediately took his rightful place just outside the front door, and Betty followed closely.

Betty didn't have much to do with Greg immediately and for a week or so kept close to her own kind just by the door, but one morning there she was at the bottom of the stairs waiting to go out with him to feed the animals. Boots on and his old jacket donned, she was there by his side, she was his friend forever.

These were two well trained guard dogs and to Mari's voice Ace did exactly as he was told and to Greg's commands so did Betty, how bright and intelligent they were. However, the two dogs spent a lot of time watching the gap on the top field, which prevented any trespassers nipping over the wall. The dogs looked fierce, but they were there to guard as they had been taught. They sat there ready to bark at any intruders, and paced to and fro from one end of the gap to the other and send them back over the wall.

"You did a good job there Elsa; you have made two people very happy" and as if it was a natural thing to do he kissed her lightly on her lips.

"I wasn't expecting to do that "he said kissing her again

"Ah but you must remember that I saw them first so they have made three people happy, so maybe we could share Betty"? Who was lying asleep close to Greg?

"All this time here you were staring me in the face, and all this time I loved you"

He did admit that he had noticed how pretty she was, but tried to dismiss the feelings as Gilbert had shown such an interest in her that he would not spoil things for his pal so he kept his distance. Now the long lingering kiss had sealed their relationship, and Betty hid her face with her paws as they made love.

Gilbert soon got over the shock although he had realized that there was more to Elsa and Greg, than Elsa and Gilbert. Mari knew that Elsa was in love with Greg as she had confided in her some time ago but would not interfere in a love triangle, it remained a secret between two women until Greg was ready to make his move, 'let love take its course they will find their own way to solve it'.

Besides, Greg might have had a hankering for London so what would have been the point of falling in love.

Summer soon turned to Autumn, Kate was in love with the local bobby and would be married next spring. They would live in the village in the police house next to the 'Spar' shop, but she still wanted to keep the small knitting shed, as she was now designing and knitting for high class shops in the UK and abroad. She labelled her products 'From the Knitting Barn' with a picture of the shed drawn and designed by Greg of course. She had employed two knitters to help her, especially as she had branched out and her little enterprise was a success.

Gilbert, Ah yes Gilbert! The potter as Greg called him, he was also interested in knitting or was it Alice, a young knitter that Kate had taught and employed. He gave her a lift to work every morning and things developed from there, they spent most of their evenings during the winter months in the pig sty ...converted of course to a nice little pad for two and called "The Piggery- Pokery".

Then one evening Kate's husband came by with a team of plain clothes officers. It was to talk to Greg and Mari.

"The dogs again" Mari thought "or Barry" but their errand was not entirely about the dogs, although they were indirectly involved.

"We've come to ask you if we could use the gap on the top field now that the busy season is over. You see, we have been keeping an eye on Barry Wright for some time, and the mischief he has caused you and the villagers gave us an excuse to visit him from time to time and suss out his place as best we could without arousing too much suspicion. We recently had a tip off about his beef burger van, and that he is also selling a bit of the white stuff from the back of his van so to speak, but that's not all. One night when we kept surveillance from the forest at the edge of your field two big dogs came bounding towards, us frightened the hell out of us though. They did not attack and simply laid down to Sgt' Bob's command, well there was no stopping the pair from seeking, and guess what they found?

Just under the old monkey puzzle tree next to the old Mr and Mrs Wright's grave was another hidden dug out space, a trap door concealed under the bush. The sacred patch where they were buried was also a secret hiding place for Barry's loot. Locked securely of course, forbidden territory and well hidden, with a sign on the little fence 'Mr and Mrs Wright...peace Mom and Dad', a forbidding sign insincerely put I think, nevertheless it prevented anyone from going any closer as a mark of respect. Except for the dogs that could not read and scratched and scraped until the earth moved and with some cutters, we opened the lock. There it was in four biscuit tins wrapped neatly in polythene, and obviously checked regularly. Thousands of pounds; must be at least forty thousand or more.

We have left it there for the time being, but we must catch Barry 'at it' and we suspect that this is why he wants access through your farm to allow his mates to come by. We need to look inside his greenhouse too, well hidden 'round the back of the stables. Your dogs started to sniff around and picked up a scent but we couldn't allow them to go too close to the yards as they have dogs of their own. Besides a light came on in the kitchen and we had to retreat, and with a sharp call from Bob and recollections of their past your dog soon came back, we were too close to take a chance... Your dog's being a bit friendly 'n all.
 Barry's dogs might have ripped them to shreds.
 There is talk about dog fights too, but when we get him we will get the lot.
 Tip off...but who, surely not Gilbert? And Greg wouldn't, no matter what.
 Can we use the gate and come up through the forest...and Oh yes, thanks for the use of your dogs"?
 Brutus knew the way to Barry's place, and had led the new twosome by way of his scent; even though he was only there in spirit, a sniff and a scratch they followed the scent, so every dog has his day... according to Mari. After a great discussion and thought, Mari said yes to the plan but not to take the dogs as Barry would know of the involvement. They were to let Gilbert know where or when they would strike so that the dogs would be kept in and not raise the alarm.
 Greg did not want Mari to be involved and if there was any blame then they were to come to him for answers. Barry would surely suspect him of informing the police after the confrontation at the train station, but Greg was not the one to blame although delighted at the prospect of seeing him cuffed and put in a police car instead of his fine Ferrari.
 There was no further mention of Barry and his white stuff, in fact Kate kept schtum about it even though her and her policeman husband might have discussed it over breakfast, but they had other things to talk about, a baby was due in the autumn so Barry was not an important topic in their life.

Grandparents were looking forward to the event and a possible christening the following spring. Maybe at the farm when the lilac would be in bloom and the apple blossom bursts out in pink and white on the bough of the trees. It would be such a picturesque and happy place for an event like that just as it was when Kate married her policeman. That was a fine do with a guard of honour of six policemen lined up to greet them at the door. Perhaps Gilbert and Sarah would be godparents

"And what about you Greg, have you asked Elsa to marry you?"

A question that went unanswered... Greg would do it in his own time and place.

'Keep the dogs in'.

That was the request; 'we will be on your land at 5 tomorrow morning, the cars will be well away from the farm, but if you can make sure that the animals are safe just in case Barry or anyone else involved tries to do a runner'. That was the news that Gilbert conveyed as they drank their tea and dunked their biscuits. Ace listened, he knew that the thrill of the chase was imminent, and he wanted to be there. Betty on the other hand could not feel the urgency to get involved, she had become the more placid of the two dogs now that she was retired from police duty.

An early start on that Thursday morning, although, as usual the animals had not yet stirred, the rest of the family were on high alert knowing what was to happen very soon, but they must not open the door to let the dogs out. There were some dull lights far in the distance and Greg wondered if they were there already, but it could have been poachers or just an early dog walker but that idea was soon dismissed as the torch lights came closer.

Mari had not stirred yet and Greg was almost tempted to take a look outside, but then the whole plan could be ruined by one false move. There were no more lights, no code, no flash from one to another. The forest was dark there were no sounds except for Ace's rustle to get amongst it and scratching at the door. Not even a quick pee this morning Ace, so cross your legs till it's over.

The police moved stealthily over the stone wall and the gap that was widened just in case they had to get a car closer to the action. Six or more uniformed police and detectives dressed in black made their way towards Barry's farm; and it remained quiet. They already had the evidence they needed in the form of two youngsters that had stopped at Barry's buffet bar a couple of months ago, and exchanged cash for the hash that was concealed between the wrappers covering the beef burger. Tasty to say the least, little did Barry suspect that this would be the last time he would be serving up his large portions of chips, and little did he think that these lads that he trusted and he had served were actually two young detectives from another town, geared up with a camera and a microphone to catch a criminal.

All that was needed now was to charge Barry and show him what they had found in the small paddock close to the house, the very same place that the dear old folk had been laid to rest many years ago. Barry's game was over. But they had to be quiet in case Barry was alerted.

A dog barked from within the stable block, and then one of the horses became fractious and whinnied hearing the dull sounds close by.

They were too late to turn back so they went forward as planned.

A light went on in the bedroom and one of the officers was caught in the floodlight that streamed from the security light over the back door... Barry had seen them.

Screams and shouts followed then the door slammed, he had escaped through the front with no consideration for wife and family who had to face the music and the long arm of the law that had barged in through the back. The roar of the red Ferrari zipped down the drive away from the officers that sat in their car at the top of his drive; the police car was headed in the opposite direction and was unprepared for the red monster that was making its escape through the gates that opened, stopping briefly to allow Barry to pass at his command, it was just like parting of the waves. There was just this one police car situated on the side of the road but pointing in the wrong direction to follow, there was enough of a gap for the red car to pass and as there had been no warning...the officers were unprepared for this sudden red streak flying past.

It was Ace;

Ace was alert and prepared; no one could stop him, he was keen to go and smelled the scent from when he had been to the farm the time before. He jumped out of Greg's bedroom window onto the low roof then into the yard and away across the field, passed Sarah's horses and into the narrow road the led to Barry's palace. After all nobody told him that he couldn't go through the bedroom window, the door was the only barrier as far as anyone was aware, forgetting about the window that was partly open then with one leap he was out onto the low roof.

Ace was led by another dog's trail, not visual to any human but had streaked ahead of him to the gate. Brutus was there to guide him and be at his side. They met on the road. Ace and the Ferrari locking jaws as the red one came closer. It was a stand-off, between the beasts and the fast approaching car.

Ace was determined not to move, so there he stood black against the headlights that blinded him, suddenly there was a yelp, and the red car flew off the road into the ditch that had caught Barry unawares once before, the Ferrari was no match for the animal that was trained to kill, and there he stood over Barry until he heard a command to 'leave'.

Then came the police car armed with the men in black, but the job was already done.

He was hurt, Ace's leg took a while to heal and the deep gash on his head would be a reminder of his bravery for ever, but it didn't matter, he was safe and he had done his job, as Brutus had instructed. Mari believed that Brutus went with him that night, guided him along to the road and to the scent. But then Mari believed in Brutus.

When the stunned Barry came 'round, he was sure that there were two dogs in his headlights. "I know there were two, I saw two dogs I tell ya", He was haunted by this experience, and repeated the same thing over and over again.

"Poppycock, it was just one dog surely!"

Every dog has its day, and Betty slept on in her comfy chair, just cocking her ears now and then...she had not moved, so what two dogs?

Soon Rhandir-Mwyn was up for sale. Barry would be away from there for a long time and without the cash from the hash they could not keep up appearances.

Rose moved on with the beef burger van and a caravan and a wad of cash she had stashed. She was a cute kid and was going to set up with plans of her own, a legit business this time. A fish 'n chips restaurant, the best money would buy She could no longer live with the lies that her father lived. She was the informer, although Barry never knew.

Eventually the house was sold to a very nice young couple, with three children who went riding with Sarah, the ornate front gates were replaced with a nice wooden one that opened and closed with a push and a click. All was quiet on the top field except for the horses that grazed, and came to the wall for tit-bits. Mari rocked in her chair and knitted baby clothes.

Greg married his Elsa having proposed in the back of his old Jenny, which jerked for the last time.

Some years later Greg and Elsa had three boys, Jake who followed in his father's footsteps and took an interest in Art, he was keen to see the world in an old van.

Bill loved to help on the farm during the summer holidays, and wanted to be a chef one day.

Arthur was the baby, and was going nowhere yet.

Jerky Jenny was restored into a beautiful lady with a new look, no more crudely drawn psychedelic art work, she was now a vision in pink. She had worked her magic, and now spent her life in the yard where the boys had their tea parties and sleep-overs. She had brought him here to Mari's house, and together they had created happiness all 'round; there was no need for memories.

They were all there in his paintings and drawings, which were sold world–wide.

The boy that once walked alone down a dark road was no longer alone.

The little lady that could hardly see over the window of his van; The house that once needed painting; roses that climbed high 'round the door onto the roof, and the crooked gate that needed repairing, and now swung with ease.

His friends;

Mel and Ross that visited from time to time.

The Vagabonds; who once sat around together, drinking beer and eating chips...were fond memories

As he skimmed again through all of these drawings there was one of a small boy climbing out of a bedroom window onto a tin roof, with one wellie on the right foot when it should have been on the left, and the other stuck in the gutter, as he made his getaway through the half open gate and a new life.

'Was that me?' he wondered, and looked over the rim of his glasses then poured himself a glass of Mari's best gooseberry wine and carried on with yet another masterpiece.

ABOUT THE AUTHOR

There is no place like home they say, and this is what prompted me to write.

Like most of us these days we have traveled. Done the sun, sand and sangria, and burnt our skin to an unhealthy orange on the hot sands of Tenerife, walked up steps and ridden on donkeys in Greece to get the best views. Camels in Cairo, that kneeled down low to let you ride a bumpy ride. Cruising in the Med with people you just met, and indeed those days were the best, but for me the best of all is the touch down in Manchester airport, and the rain lashing like stair rods on the tarmac, Feet getting soaked because you are still wearing flip-flops, legs tingling from the cold air. Scurrying for the luggage and finding the transport that takes you home.

The key in the lock, the dogs that bark on your arrival pleased to see you after a long, long week away. To hear the familiar sound of the kettle and enjoy a good cup of tea with milk that tastes like milk.

All these things make you look around and appreciate the wonders of Wales. The cool sand of Newborough beach, to drink a glass of wine in a small tavern on the beach in Y Felinheli and taste the salt in a dish of mussels, to sit awhile experiencing and enjoying the view high up in the Tryfan mountains and the scenery before you.

It's so nice to go traveling but…

Margaret B
Born and bred in Wales, in a small village close to Moel Tryfan mountain. An aspiring author and teller of tales.